T0016194

MASTER OF
THE BATHHOUSE
SPICE AND WOLF
LAWRENCE

MISTRESS OF
THE BATHHOUSE
SPICE AND WOLF
HOLO THE WISEWOLF

"FATHER!
BROTHER!
HURRY UP!"

DAUGHTER OF
THE WISEWOLF
AND THE MERCHANT
MYURI

"It rained not long ago, no? The mountains should be ripe with mushrooms."

SUMMER'S HARVEST AND WOLF

THE COLOR OF DAWN AND WOLF

"Farewell," Elsa said briefly, and began walking down the road, headed south.

It had been two days since the festival in Salonia had ended, and as the morning came once again, a reluctant air filled the town, a hint that the townsfolk would begrudgingly return to their daily lives in preparation for winter.

Devout Priestess
ELSA

SPICE & WOLF

VOL. 23

SPRING LOG VI

By Isuna Hasekura
Illustrated by Jyuu Ayakura

LORD OF THE
VALLAN BISHOPRIC
RAHDEN

THE GEM OF THE
SEA AND WOLF

"SULTO! WHY DID YOU LEAVE ME
BEHIND IN THE VILLAGE?!"
"LORD RAHDEN! WHY ARE YOU—"
AS SULTO BEGAN TO SPEAK, A YOUNG
BOY PEEKED OUT FROM BESIDE THE
FURIOUS RAHDEN.

SQUIRREL SPIRIT
WHO LIVES IN A
CURSED MOUNTAIN
TANYA

Contents

VOLUME XXIII
SPRING LOG VI

ISUNA HASEKURA
JYUU AYAKURA

YEN
ON

NEW YORK

SPICE AND WOLF, Volume 23
ISUNA HASEKURA

Translation by Jasmine Bernhardt
Cover art by Jyuu Ayakura

OKAMI TO KOSHINRYO
©Isuna Hasekura 2021
Edited by Dengeki Bunko
First published in Japan in 2021 by KADOKAWA CORPORATION, Tokyo.
English translation rights arranged with KADOKAWA CORPORATION, Tokyo, through TUTTLE-MORI AGENCY, INC., Tokyo.

English translation © 2022 by Yen Press, LLC

Yen On
150 West 30th Street, 19th Floor
New York, NY 10001

Visit us at yenpress.com
facebook.com/yenpress
twitter.com/yenpress
yenpress.tumblr.com
instagram.com/yenpress

First Yen On Edition: November 2022
Edited by Yen Press Editorial: Payton Campbell, Ivan Liang
Designed by Yen Press Design: Wendy Chan

Yen On is an imprint of Yen Press, LLC.
The Yen On name and logo are trademarks of Yen Press, LLC.

Library of Congress Cataloging-in-Publication Data
Names: Hasekura, Isuna, 1982– author. | Ayakura, Jū, 1981– illustrator. | Bernhardt, Jasmine, translator.
Title: Spring log VI / Isuna Hasekura, Jyuu Ayakura ; translation by Jasmine Bernhardt.
Other titles: Spring log. English
Description: First Yen On edition. | New York, NY : Yen On, 2022. | Series: Spice & Wolf ; 23
Identifiers: LCCN 2022034874 | ISBN 9781975348649 (trade paperback)
Subjects: CYAC: Fantasy. | Goddesses—Fiction. | Wolves—Fiction. | LCGFT: Light novels.
Classification: LCC PZ7.H2687 Srk 2022 | DDC [Fic]—dc23
LC record available at https://lccn.loc.gov/2022034874

ISBNs: 978-1-9753-4864-9 (paperback)
       978-1-9753-4865-6 (ebook)

10 9 8 7 6 5 4 3 2 1

LSC-C

Printed in the United States of America

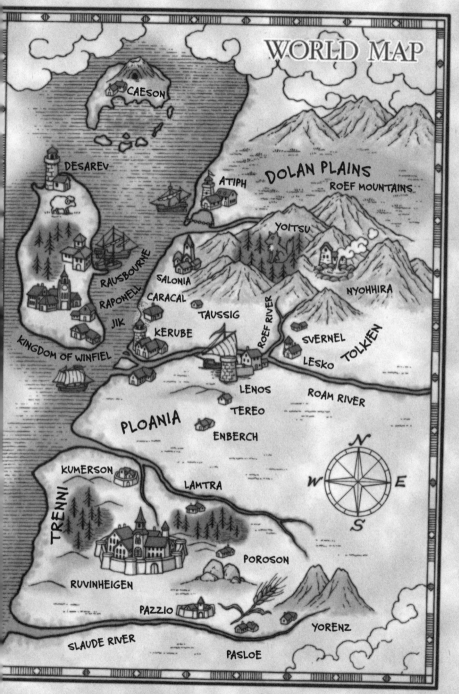

WORLD MAP

CAESON

DESAREV

ATIPH

DOLAN PLAINS

ROEF MOUNTAINS

YOITSU

RAUSBOURNE

SALONIA

NYOHHIRA

RAPONELL

CARACAL

JIK

TAUSSIG

KERUBE

ROEF RIVER

SVERNEL

LESKO

TOLKIEN

KINGDOM OF WINFIEL

LENOS

TEREO

ROAM RIVER

PLOANIA

ENBERCH

N

W E

S

KUMERSON

LAMTRA

TRENNI

POROSON

RUVINHEIGEN

PAZZIO

YORENZ

SLAUDE RIVER

PASLOE

Map Illustration: Hidetada Idemitsu

THE GEM OF THE SEA AND WOLF

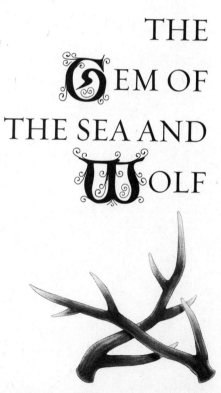

If one were to take the form of a bird and fly over Salonia, it would look as though clusters of mushrooms were growing atop a gold-and-brown carpet. The town thrived on inland trade, and that was the sort of place it was.

It was once a vacant piece of land, used only by local farming villages for bartering produce, but that changed when a wandering priest appeared one day and built a hermitage on the spot. For the first time the area had a place of worship, so locals visited more frequently, which in turn drew the business of merchants, which then caused walls to be built, inns to open, and roads to be paved. And so, a town was born.

Salonia was known for its biannual market; the market this autumn was quite exciting, as it typically was.

Though successful at a glance, the truth was that the foundations of the market had been struggling beneath a weighty problem, a result of which caused several individuals to find themselves tossed in jail.

As the townsfolk bemoaned their concerns, a few travelers who had come to town conjured up a solution to the problem. The solution was so close to magic that it ended up recorded in the town annals.

As trouble settled on the hearts of the people of Salonia, a strange traveling couple came to town… was how that particular record began.

The husband claimed to be an ordinary retired traveling merchant, but before arriving in Salonia he had solved a mystery involving a place that was considered a cursed mountain and sold it to the Debau Company for a high price. This sharp retired merchant had erased the debts plaguing the people of the town without using a single coin.

Though possessed of an exceedingly rare sense of judgment, he always deferred to his young wife, and the people of Salonia often saw how tight a hold she had on him.

It was not long after that the townsfolk began to whisper among themselves—perhaps his mercantile prowess was owed to his wife. The rumors likely stemmed from the strangely domineering aura she possessed, despite her young looks.

The girl had flaxen hair, reddish-amber eyes, spoke like people of ages past, and was crafty yet sweet.

She was a fantastic drinker, besting every man in town who came to challenge her, so of course the former merchant in question was no match for her, either.

The pair had come to town at the beginning of autumn, and once they had made a vivid show of solving Salonia's problem, they enjoyed their stay in town. May God watch over them…

Once she finished reading the draft of the town's annals, Holo's nostrils flared with pride.

Lawrence, who had sat beside her reading the same text, could not help but speak up with a strained smile.

"Why did they write more of you than me?"

"I am Holo the Wisewolf. The author knows well."

Despite appearing to be an ordinary young woman, the truth was that Holo sported pointed wolf ears on her head and a fluffy tail growing from her backside—she was a wolf spirit, several centuries old.

She had once been regarded as a deity, and an average bathhouse owner such as Lawrence could hardly compare; her pride was only natural.

Holo had come to enjoy recording her day-to-day in a diary, but there was a considerable difference between what she wrote down herself and what others wrote.

"Can we not have a painting made of this?"

She had gotten a taste of that luxury with the mural in the port town of Atiph.

"No painting can fully convey your beauty," Lawrence replied.

Holo was delighted at first, but she pouted at him when she realized he had tricked her.

They stared at each other in silence, but before long, both broke out into smiles.

"Why don't we grab something to eat when we go turn this draft back in?"

"Aye, I do crave fish every once in a while."

She had also gotten a taste for fresh fish in Atiph.

Lawrence wanted to check the weight of his purse, but he noticed how Holo was reaching for him.

He grasped her hand, and she beamed at him.

How could he resist when she smiled at him like that?

Lawrence laughed to himself—the annals were right after all. They left their room at the inn together.

As Lawrence and Holo made their way to the church to return the draft, they found a crowd of people pouring from the building; noon mass had just ended. Several merchants noted Lawrence's presence and tipped their hats in greeting. He felt a bit embarrassed having become such a celebrity, but Holo, on the other hand, was eating it up.

It was almost as though she was saying that she was the one who had made him.

"Oh, Mister Lawrence."

"Hello, Miss Elsa."

When the pair stepped inside the church, they came across a priestess with her hair pulled back tightly in a bun, carrying a heavy stack of scripture.

She was an old acquaintance he had encountered not long after meeting Holo, on the road in search of Holo's home.

Not only that, but Elsa had officiated their wedding as well; that, combined with her shrewd personality, made her the number two person who Lawrence would listen to without question—number one being Holo, of course.

"We've come to return the draft. It was a little embarrassing reading all of that."

"That simply means you did a fine job. I can still scarcely believe you pulled it off."

Lawrence had freed people from their debt without a single piece of silver changing hands. It sounded like magic when put that way, but when it came down to it, solving the underlying issue had not been all that outlandish.

Lawrence handed over the sheaf of papers, and Elsa accepted it with great care, as though there were still secrets hidden inside.

"The aftermath was the greater headache for you, wasn't it, Miss Elsa?"

Once word spread about the way Lawrence erased debt, naturally, others began to wonder if they could do the same with their own debt. But debt was a questionable topic, and since the job entailed undoing the chain that linked everyone together, that meant the Salonia church sat at the center of it all. It was at this stage that Elsa had been called on to take charge—she was not only good with writing and numbers, but the strength of her faith was beyond doubt.

"Resolved in three days with much enthusiasm. It was not that big of a problem."

Her clear honey-colored eyes made it obvious she was not saying that just to make him, or herself, feel better.

Lawrence bowed his head, impressed, when Elsa spoke up again.

"That reminds me," she said. "A carriage brought in something rather interesting this morning. I was hoping to give it to the both of you."

What she said caught the attention of Holo, who had been mid-yawn. Elsa handed them a booklet she had been carrying with her hefty scriptures.

"Selected passages from the Twilight Cardinal's vernacular translation of the scripture. I think it has been wonderfully translated."

There was an uncharacteristic teasing tone to the way she said *Twilight Cardinal*.

And the reason she had called the booklet "interesting" was not because she was a devout priestess.

The person who immediately came to mind was a young man whom Lawrence knew well: Col. The "Twilight Cardinal" was the title the world knew him by.

Elsa was one of Col's teachers—she had instilled in him the habit of saying grace at meals when he was a child. She must have found it so strange and touching that the little boy had grown up to do such great things.

Lawrence was no less proud to see that the little boy he happened to take in on his journey had grown up to be such a renowned individual. He was even slightly jealous.

As he took the booklet, enjoying the comings and goings of all the different emotions inside him, Holo stuck her face closer to the book and gave it a sniff.

"What? 'Tis not a letter from them?"

"No. I do ask the merchants who come through to keep an eye out for their whereabouts, but…I hear all sorts of stories, about being in this town or another, or battling with corrupt clergy in another region, or—no, no, they were debating priests up on the mountain! They've become somewhat of a myth; everyone is making up their own stories about them. Becoming this famous has its ups and downs."

Col had left the hot spring village of Nyohhira to pursue his dream of becoming a man of the cloth.

It did not take long for him to throw himself into an adventure that would make such waves throughout the world, and Lawrence was as concerned as ever about where the boy was and what he was doing in that moment.

"No news is good news," Holo declared. "And to hold such a thing in our hands means he is once again holing himself up in his room, munching on onions to stave off drowsiness."

She took the booklet, shaking it, making the pages flap.

"Can you not imagine the little fool sitting beside him, utter boredom on her face?"

When a mischievous smile crossed Holo's face, Lawrence pursed his lips.

As she watched, Elsa commented with a smile, "Some refer to her as Saint Myuri. Constantly smiling, merciful as the sun."

When he heard that, Lawrence was not sure if he should smile or sigh.

The biggest reason he wanted to know where they were and what they were up to was not only because Col was like a son to him, but more so that his only daughter, Myuri, had latched onto him and followed him when he departed.

8

Letters had occasionally trickled in after they left, but soon they arrived less and less frequently, and had now come to a complete stop. His worry that something had happened to them had only grown.

First, there was the fear that trouble had befallen them somewhere along their journey.

There was also the matter that while Col and Myuri were not related by blood, they were still ostensibly brother and sister. Lawrence often wondered if something had changed in their relationship.

"That little fool never knows when to give up."

"I have three boys, but if you told me that one of them was going to live with his wife in a city far away, I would certainly be sad."

"Indeed. Though one could easily visit or ask him to send all the delicious delicacies his new home has to offer."

"That is also true."

Views between the serious and honest Elsa and the old, crude Holo often clashed, but it was on these topics that they saw eye to eye.

"Come now, husband. Get it together. We have a job to do—namely getting ready for the festival that concludes the market."

Holo whacked Lawrence on the back with the booklet.

"What? You just want to drink."

"Fool. No one in this town can drink more than I can. The responsibility of choosing what drinks will be served at the festival obviously falls to me."

Even Elsa, who would typically interject with words about moderation in times like these, refrained from saying anything; this particular instance of drinking was an actual job, after all.

"We argue every year over which granary to choose, so having Miss Holo choose for us this year should be a great help."

"See?"

Holo lifted her chin in pride, and both Lawrence and Elsa sighed.

"This isn't just your everyday wine. This is distilled barley liquor. Don't drink too much."

"You fool. When have I ever told you I have had too much to drink?"

Considering how she could proclaim such a thing loudly in a church meant that no scolding from Lawrence or Elsa would reach her ears.

"What snacks would go well with it, I wonder? Jerky, perhaps—cured with smoke strong enough to make one choke... Or honeyed candies? I find those rather irresistible."

Lawrence could tell she was in high spirits when he saw how her tail swished beneath her clothes.

"Dear?"

"I know, I know. We'll see you later, Miss Elsa."

"Yes, take care."

A somewhat exasperated, yet envious smile crossed Elsa's face as Holo dragged Lawrence away.

Several hours later, Lawrence carried a pleasantly drunk Holo on his back as they returned to the inn.

When Salonia's spring and autumn markets open, merchants come from all over—not just the immediate surrounding area.

The end of the autumn market was always marked with a festival that gives thanks for the harvest and prays for a good crop the following year.

When Lawrence used to travel around as a merchant, he of course attended all sorts of local festivals, but was always conflicted with himself when it came to taking advantage of the hearty festival atmosphere to sell goods at inflated prices, so he could never fully enjoy himself. In practice he kept his head down, striving to walk one step farther than his competitors, to beat them out to the next destination.

His hurried travels only slowed once he started traveling with Holo.

It was then that he started to appreciate the scenery, to truly realize how the air smelled for the first time.

The festival preparations were much the same; he only understood that *this* was the most exciting time for the townsfolk when Holo grabbed his hand.

"This is a good place; they have all sorts of grain here."

Holo, whose hangover had finally subsided come nightfall, spoke as she sat at one of the tables outside their inn, nursing a cup of alcohol despite the previous day's activities.

That said, she slowly sipped at it like it was a watered-down cider, so perhaps she was not totally oblivious to the lessons learned here.

"Business went well for me. I guess the townsfolk feel much lighter without any of that debt weighing them down."

"Mm. And you sold all that fetid nonsense in the back of the cart?"

Lawrence had to use his fame somehow now that he had made something of a name for himself in town. He had managed to sell half of the mountain of sulfur powder he had brought with them when they left Nyohhira. He even thought he might be able to sell a bit more, considering how the townsfolk, in their debt-free joy, were talking about making impromptu hot springs by digging holes and filling them with hot water.

"I've no complaints, then," Holo said, comfortably closing her eyes, allowing the cool evening breeze play with her bangs.

There was still time before the sun completely set, but the town did not go to sleep in the evening when the festival loomed near. As Lawrence sat hoping that Holo, who had spent most of her day napping, would not drink too much today, the innkeeper brought them food and warm soup.

"Ah, yes, there is nothing better than this after having a bit too much to drink," she said, eagerly slurping the mushrooms and vegetables that had been boiled with the broth. "But I do have one regret."

"Hmm?"

Holo set down her bowl of soup, instead picking up a slender, seared sardine and biting into its head.

"At least 'tis not herring. I heard that this town would typically have a rich selection of river fish to choose from."

Herring was so abundant in the ocean that it was said a person could stab a sword into the water and pull it out skewered with the fish; one could always find it on the dinner tables of houses far inland. Not only that, it was cheap—and so it became a staple during the winter, and even those who were not as picky with food as Holo often detested it.

In contrast, fish from rivers so dark one could scarcely see any at all were often far away from the sea and the salt needed to preserve said fish, so they never went far. Good, local river fish could only be eaten in those specific places.

"I took a look at the river by the town, but it didn't seem like there were a whole lot of fish in there. And you know what they say—the two things that will always find you away from the seashores are the moon and herring. But this is a sardine anyway."

Lawrence bit into the fish, and a delightful bitterness filled his mouth.

He would have preferred it seared just a little more, but Holo drew up her shoulders.

"Look, you see the hazy mountain in the distance? From our room at the inn?"

"Hmm? Oh, yeah."

As Lawrence reached out for his third sardine, wanting more of that bitterness in his mouth, Holo smacked his hand away.

"'Tis not the way we came into town, and I hear there is a mythical pond tucked away there."

"Mythical?" Lawrence repeated, not paying too much mind as he spoke; he lifted and waved in the air the plate that once housed the sardines at the innkeeper.

"They say the most delicious trout lives there, but there is not a single one in stock in any of the stores this year, of all years."

"Huh."

Being the bathhouse owner that he was, Lawrence began to think of a meal he could serve with trout—it tasted great wrapped in a large tree leaf and fried with mushrooms and plenty of butter.

"They were apparently raising them especially in that pond, but then a disease struck them."

"Rearing fish in a pond, huh? It's not like making a preserve in a river at all; it's much more difficult. They say everyone in Nyohhira's tried it a few times before, but it's never gone well."

"And that is why all we eat is herring and sardines."

Despite her complaints, Holo greedily munched on the sardines that Lawrence had gotten for himself.

A plump trout, of course, went well with a mug of ale.

And as a former businessman, Lawrence did have some thoughts on the matter.

"That must feel pretty bad. They must have been raising them specifically for the festival season."

A mountain fishpond was surely a precious source of income to the locals. They might hesitate in putting even more fish in the

14

pond after a disease had wiped the previous lot out, and he could easily foresee their troubles continuing.

As those thoughts crossed his mind, Holo's eyes darted away, as though her gaze had been drawn elsewhere. Lawrence followed her eyes to find Elsa, giving them a small wave.

"What does she want?"

Holo's question was thorny because she knew that once Elsa joined them at the dinner table, the woman's scolding and lectures would accompany her.

Maybe Elsa had caught wind that Holo had ultimately knocked herself out drinking after selecting the alcohol that would be served at the festival.

"As a devout servant of God, it is ever my duty to preach moderation to you," Elsa began, exasperation coloring her voice, as she turned her attention to Lawrence. "But my business today is with Mister Lawrence. I have a request to ask of you."

"Of me?" he asked.

At that moment, the innkeeper brought out more seared sardines; Holo reached out not only to grab the freshly-seared sardines, but also to grab the scruff of Lawrence's neck.

"These are mine. I will need some collateral because you will be working too hard."

The same thing had been written in the annals, so Lawrence would not protest. He drew himself inward, just like the sardines that Holo was mercilessly decapitating with her teeth.

"You will need to provide some collateral, too." Elsa turned to Holo.

"Hmm?"

"Wouldn't you like to eat some delicious trout?"

Speak of the devil.

Lawrence and Holo exchanged glances before listening to what Elsa had to say.

15

*   *   *

The mountain Holo saw from the inn window was, reportedly, part of territory called the Rahden Bishopric.

It was nowhere near as vast as the Vallan Bishopric, where the pair had solved the mystery of the cursed mountain with Elsa; all it had was one small village. This remote, mountain hamlet was unusual for the area in that it ran a river-fish nursery. Their fattened trout were especially well-received, and they were considered a delicacy in Salonia, since all the townsfolk could fish from their muddy nearby river were carp. Disease had plagued the nursery for several years now, and it had been particularly bad this year—every fish had perished. Their only choice was to wait until the pond water was rejuvenated, and it would be a long time before the trout would grace Salonia's dinner tables once again.

When Elsa finished her explanation, Lawrence guessed that she would next ask them to use their mercantile prowess to save them from the tough situation.

But with their main industry gone, it would be difficult to find something else to replace it and put money in their pockets and food on their tables. Lawrence could establish a trade empire if he could solve something like that in the blink of an eye. As those thoughts crossed his mind, he found that what Elsa had to ask of him was somewhat similar to what he was expecting, but entirely different at the same time.

"You want me to find a way to get them a loan?"

The villagers were likely troubled by the loss of their main industry, so a loan was logical.

"Would you like me to speak to a company somewhere? I'm not sure if I could…"

Loans meant a long-term relationship between lender and

borrower. Anyone in their right mind would hesitate to give money to a traveler who suddenly turned up one day with haphazard excuses. And it was not long ago that Salonia had been caught in such a tangled web of debts that the town had been virtually paralyzed.

As Lawrence considered how he had *just* untangled said web, Elsa shook her head.

"Not at all. Companies have already turned the village down, and their only option is the Church."

"..."

He did not respond right away because what Elsa was saying sounded so strange to him.

Even if Elsa was, quite literally, in a temporary position, she still held the post of pastor. And not only that, she had played her own part in resolving the commotion that had overtaken the town, which meant she likely had more sway than her post should have afforded her.

It was God's will that she help those in need, so if she expressed her desire to help those people, she could likely convince the Church with ease.

"Or would you like me to investigate whether they're able to repay any debts?"

Elsa always stood with her back perfectly straight, every strand of hair in her bun perfectly in place even after a long day of work.

Uncharacteristically, the woman seemed to hunch her shoulders slightly as she said, "No, that is not a problem. The nursery had been doing poorly for years now, but since the villagers are diligent, they have now made stable lives for themselves hunting deer and making leather string. This town is a hub of trade—no amount of leather straps to secure bags shut would ever be enough. That is why I doubt they truly need a loan after all. What I mean to ask is..." Elsa turned to Lawrence, her typically tough demeanor now colored by a hue of concern on her face. "We want you to find a *way for the Church to loan money to them*."

The unease on Elsa's face made it seem as though she was a young child trying to speak a foreign language.

It truly seemed as though she had no confidence that what she was trying to say made any sense.

"Er, I ask that you find a way—"

"No, I understand. It'll be fine," Lawrence replied.

It seemed as though Elsa wanted to say more, but she meekly kept her mouth shut.

But while Lawrence understood each and every word she said, he did not quite understand the sum of their meaning. After a brief silence, Holo spoke up.

"The villagers want money, no?" "And you Church people want to loan them money, no? It sounds quite fair to me."

The look on her face told them that she was already fed up with the inevitable complications that were to come. She knew there was a catch.

Elsa placed her hand to her chest and took several deep breaths, carefully choosing her words before speaking up.

"Personally, I empathize with the reasons why the villagers are asking for money. I believe the Church should help them. However..." She turned her attention toward Lawrence, an apologetic look on her face. "However, the Church lending out money is not an agreeable thing. And we are in the midst of a storm that questions all the evil acts the Church has committed."

She looked apologetic because she had no intention of criticizing Lawrence and Holo for such a thing.

Holo overtly turned her gaze away; that was because Col and Myuri had been sending considerable shock waves through the Church, and dust had been stirred up all over the world.

It was a good thing that all the years of wrongdoing the Church had committed were being held to account, but unfortunately, not everything about it would resolve in a peaceable manner. The Church was hypocritical—despite how much it praised asceticism, it had grown fat from all the tithes and donations it had received over the years.

And so, in recent times, anything regarding the Church and its money would be scrutinized, and anything that might seem innocent at first was often met with dubious looks.

Ultimately, the reason why things had turned out this way could very likely be because of Col.

"Well, if it is the right thing to do, then it shouldn't be a problem for you to lend them money, right? I'm sure it won't go against Church teachings so long as the interest rate isn't too high."

It was moneylenders that the Church found fault with; the scripture said that if one were to borrow a room for the night, the debt must be repaid. Theologians often interpreted this as meaning that a gesture of thanks was permissible repayment in the eyes of God.

"Tacit approval, if anything. But the priests here are hesitant—they think we may be set up as a scapegoat for something."

Lawrence could understand that.

"They believe that any excess money loaned to them will be met with suspicion, especially since the village is not particularly troubled by money."

"If that be the reason why you will not lend them money, then do you have a reason why you *do* want to? It sounds as though the ones who cultivate the fish are not troubled by a lack of coin," Holo said, and Elsa turned to look at her.

She then directed her gaze ahead—the church had come into view.

"Or rather, could you listen to our situation with fresh ears and offer your judgments?"

She meant to say that the villagers' pleas were as coordinated and theatrical as a storytelling.

And Elsa was an old friend who knew exactly what Holo was.

"My ears come at the cost of a refreshingly cold mug of ale."

Holo could tell when people were lying.

Elsa's shoulders heaved with a sigh as she made her way toward the church.

The sky had turned violet by the time they reached Salonia's church; lanterns were now lit throughout town. Evening mass had ended, and while Lawrence initially thought the church might be completely shuttered at this point, they instead found the doors wide open and several women loitering by the entrance.

"There they are!"

The moment a plump woman noticed the trio, she pointed her finger and exclaimed. A crowd of people then shuffled out from inside the church. They all appeared rustic in their dress; it was unlikely they were from the town.

Lawrence was bewildered, and Holo looked dubiously at Elsa.

Elsa cleared her throat and raised her voice.

"I have brought the great merchant who saved Salonia! Make way, make way!"

"Oh, great merchant!"

"It's you!"

"Thanks be to heaven!"

Elsa literally parted the sea of people, who had gathered as though a saint had appeared.

Lawrence enjoyed himself, recalling a time when he would get into fistfights over buying goods at market, but the sensitive Holo was shocked and shrunk into herself slightly in fear.

Lawrence gripped her shoulders to offer reassurance and they followed Elsa into the church.

Inside, in the nave where the altar sat, there were men sitting however they pleased throughout the pews. And it was truly in whichever manner they pleased—some were weighing wheat, and some were even sharpening their hatchets. Some had gone shirtless, mending their clothes, and one person had even brought along several goats.

"Hey! I told you, no goats inside! Go tie them up out back and come back later!"

Upon Elsa's scolding, a man who looked much like a goat himself led the three goats out of the church.

As she stood sighing, a priest appeared from the corridor leading into the back rooms.

"Elsa, over here."

He gestured to them, and Lawrence went along with Elsa to him. Following behind them was the crowd of all of those who had been loitering outside the church and inside the nave.

When they came to stand before what looked to be a multipurpose hall, Elsa turned around and said, "You all wait here."

The command made the whole crowd—not unlike a flock of ducks—come to a halt, but they all began muttering among one another. Then, the slender, debonair bishop opened the door, allowing Lawrence, Holo, and Elsa inside; Elsa shut the door behind them, cutting the crowd off.

"What is going on?" Holo asked, like she had been having a nightmare in Lawrence's arms, and one of the people sitting at the long table stood.

"I hope my people haven't been troubling you."

21

An old man with gray hair and an earnest look on his face addressed them. Lawrence surmised that he must be the mayor of the Rahden Bishopric.

"It's all right, Mayor. Everyone is behaving themselves," the bishop said casually; he certainly sounded like he belonged in a town flourishing from trade.

"I thank you for taking in the villagers. I did not originally intend to come with all of these people..."

"It's not a problem. Any lamb of God is welcome to make themselves at home here."

The bishop paid them lip service, but it was Elsa's job to actually clean the chapel. Her face was scrunched up as though she was fighting a headache; she must have remembered the goats in the nave.

"And who might this be?"

"These two are the merchants who saved Salonia from dire straits, the ones we mentioned before."

Now suddenly the topic of the conversation, Lawrence hurriedly conjured his best merchant's smile.

"Ah, I see. I am honored." The old man lowered his head politely and introduced himself, "My name is Sulto. I act as mayor for the small village in the Rahden Bishopric."

"Kraft Lawrence. This is my wife, Holo."

When Lawrence introduced himself in turn, a relieved smile crossed Sulto's face, like he had come across a hometown acquaintance in a foreign land.

"I have heard stories of you, Sir Lawrence. No words can express my thanks that someone such as you has offered to help me. Thank you so much."

Lawrence was not sure what sort of embellished stories the old man had heard of him, so he simply gave an ambiguous smile and nodded.

"Now then, how may I be of service?"

Just as he anticipated, the man who named himself Sulto was mayor of the village famous for its trout hatchery.

According to what Elsa had told them earlier, while the church itself wanted to loan them money, current affairs made the act of lending out money a tricky one for the church. Therefore, they wanted a merchant's wisdom to find an acceptable way to offer a loan without seeming suspicious. There was good reason that the villagers had come out in force to the church.

But Lawrence had, at first, thought the village had wanted to borrow money after its hatchery industry had failed because they no longer had a way to make a living, but that did not seem to be the case. The men loitering in the nave held food that looked to have been purchased from town and owned tools that looked to be of good quality, despite their shoddy dress.

What did these villagers, who clearly led comfortable lives, want to do with the loan money, and why was the church trying to support them?

Sulto adjusted his posture under Lawrence's gaze and said, "We would like the church to loan us money so that Lord Rahden may become a bishop."

The first word that came to Lawrence's mind was *simony*. It was the bishop who then interjected.

"That wording will cause misunderstandings, Mister Mayor." He then turned to Lawrence and gave his own merchant-like smile. "Please, take a seat. There is a delicate situation unfolding in the Rahden Bishopric."

This sounded fishy to Lawrence, and so he found himself glancing in Elsa's direction. She was the ideal priest: honest and unforgiving of any crooked acts. His gaze was questioning—raising money to earn themselves a high-ranking clergyman was the very thing that would attract all the wrong kinds of attention in this day and age.

Lawrence had not done this because he was a particularly fastidious man, but because he was not fond of the idea of being made to cross a bridge he could not verify the safety of.

And surprisingly, Elsa turned to meet Lawrence's gaze head-on.

"Just listen to what he has to say."

Whatever it was, it was apparently perfectly valid under her ethical perspective.

Even Holo, who was also watching suspiciously, knew perfectly well what Elsa was like. She blinked, not expecting that reaction.

"...All right," Lawrence said, nodding. "Tell me."

Lawrence and Holo sat across from Mayor Sulto.

"Our town is situated within the Rahden Bishopric, but that is just a nickname for the area," Sulto explained. "Lord Rahden, who developed the small, poor sliver of land within the mountains, is an upstanding practitioner of God's teachings. He leads us—he is like a father to us villagers. We call our land the Rahden Bishopric in honor of his great deeds."

It sounded a lot like magnificently bearded tavern owners who were sometimes referred to as lords. Lawrence recalled a small handful of areas in his travels that had bore similar naming conventions.

"Has Lord Rahden received official benefices?"

It was the bishop who answered Lawrence's question.

"Allow me to speak on behalf of the records in Salonia." The bishop cleared his throat, beginning his statement with an odd prelude. "I suppose it was about forty years ago—the land was donated to him by the noble family that once owned it. He had served as representative for a church that reportedly once stood in the area. That does not, however, make him a member of the clergy that has received benefices."

Lawrence held back the grin that threatened to cross his face when the bishop said *a church that reportedly once stood in the area*. In translation, that meant there was a possibility that Rahden had received a donation of land while impersonating a member of the Church.

"But Lord Rahden's act did save many people," the bishop said, almost as though he had read Lawrence's mind. "Forty years ago, Salonia was the front line in the war against the pagans. Our annals state that it was a time of terrible chaos. It was then that Lord Rahden appeared, built a pond in an inhospitable mountain, raised fish, and took in people displaced by the war. Our records state that the fish from the Rahden Bishopric staved off starvation when fish could no longer be caught from the corpse-polluted rivers."

"I see."

Lawrence could see why Elsa wanted to support them.

Sulto then spoke up, impatience in his voice.

"Our home had been consumed by the war. I was young—newly married—so I took my wife and my newborn and headed for Lord Rahden's village, clinging to the rumors of salvation. When we finally made it to the village, we were exhausted, smoke still billowing from our singed clothes, and Lord Rahden greeted us by throwing us a net he had been weaving himself. I remember it like it was yesterday. He is a godsent man," Sulto said, almost in prayer, grasping the Church crest that hung around his neck.

As Lawrence watched the mayor, he slowly inhaled and held his breath. The villagers had poured into the church because all of them had experienced the same past, and they had all been saved by Rahden. Not only that, the man was not an official member of the clergy despite having done so many good deeds, and Lawrence now understood why that did not seem to sit well with the villagers. They could not stand to see Rahden without the proper accolades, so they had come to Salonia.

But accepting a benefice was commonly accompanied by bribery, so it was hard to imagine that the money borrowed for the purpose of becoming a bishop would be used for anything but.

Curious to know how that was working out, Lawrence glanced at the bishop, who gave him a knowing nod in turn.

"In terms of granting him bishophood, the pope's office has heard of Lord Rahden's faith directly. So your apprehensions of…bribery are not an issue here."

Lawrence turned to look at Elsa, and she nodded wordlessly as she pointed to her priest's stole. She was married and had children, yet she had been ordained as a priest. The Church had been tremendously shorthanded in this time of change, so they were willing to grant priesthood to anyone they could find, especially capable individuals such as herself.

They had set eyes on Rahden because they likely wanted to incorporate someone who was already well-known for his faith— someone who could easily win the hearts and minds of the people.

If that were the case, then there was one thing Lawrence did not understand.

"Then what are you planning on doing with the money?"

Sulto sighed. "We were told that if Lord Rahden were to become a bishop, then he would have to go south to the pope's office, and that might take more than a year."

Lawrence wondered if it would be used for travel and living expenses, but he had a feeling that they could raise donations in town.

"When Lord Rahden heard that, he said he would turn down the offer. He said he cannot be away from the village for over a year, that he will not leave until the village's hatchery has been made whole."

The man sounded like someone who was staunch in his obligations.

Lawrence was about to nod, impressed, but he paused. "Um… But I have heard that things are going relatively well with deer hunting and related crafts."

Surely, they could manage, even without the hatchery.

Sulto looked at Lawrence, a hint of sadness in his eyes. "You heard correctly. It's always Lord Rahden who is helping us, so we started searching in earnest for industry that could replace the hatchery long before there had been any signs of illness among the fish. And thank God, when the Vallan Bishopric, on the other side of the mountain, started growing again, that caused many deer to appear around the village. Our livelihoods are now supported by venison, deer hides, and leather straps."

The Vallan Bishopric had once been developed as a mine and had gone bare.

But Tanya, the squirrel spirit, had worked hard to replant the trees in the forest and life had returned to the area.

Lawrence, a former merchant who brought distant lands together, was delighted to learn of the link between these two places. He quietly reminded himself to tell Tanya what had happened.

"That is why we believe God was the one who brought this opportunity to him. This will allow him to be away and take a break from work in the village for a while, and his faith has been recognized to the point where he can be formally recognized as a bishop. We urged him to take it on. But he said no, that he cannot be away from the village while the hatchery's future remains uncertain. Perhaps it's because we are too inexperienced."

"So, is this a loan to help revitalize the hatchery?"

Sulto did not nod in confirmation, nor did he deny the statement.

"We want enough money that Lord Rahden can leave the village with peace of mind."

"..."

The mayor likely thought that revitalizing the trout hatchery was going to be difficult. Due to the nature of it being a pond, all the fish within the hatchery would be lost in an instant at the first signs of disease, so it was also likely that he thought it would be best not to rely so much on it in the future.

But Lawrence was painfully understanding of their motives. He did not even need to look at Holo to know that the villagers were only acting with Rahden's best interests in mind.

He understood why Elsa wanted to help, and also why the Salonia church was looking for a reason to lend a hand.

On the other hand, the truth remained that he was not sure under what pretext the church should lend them money.

In truth, it would be best if they could borrow money from one of the companies in town, but if they got wind that it was so Rahden could become a bishop, then any company would rightfully think twice.

The biggest issue was the current trend: the scrutiny under which the Church existed grew harsher day by day.

And it was very likely that the amount of money they were asking for was enough to hold sway over the entire operations of the village, so that was another reason to step back.

Lending money to someone in power was a move that required courage, because there was no guarantee that they would pay the money back. Those related to the Church especially stood out; they could easily insist it was considered a donation, and the money would never be returned.

If there was anyone who could help, it would be the Church, but if records showed that the village leader became a bishop soon after receiving the money, then others would likely point out that it was corrupt money meant for bribery.

On the surface, there was every indication of something shady going on.

"Well, Mister Lawrence? All of us here at the Salonia church would like to help the people of the Rahden Bishopric in any way we can," the bishop said, turning his attention to Lawrence. "When I asked Pastor Elsa if we might be able to secure your help in the matter, she said that you would be willing so long as there is no corruption at play."

And then Elsa found that there was no foul play, but there was a big problem. Her diagnosis had been correct.

"By corruption, you ultimately mean...that no record should remain of the church directly lending money to the village, correct?"

"Yes. It sounds like a bad thing when you put it that way, but—"

"No, I understand. Just because facial hair is natural does not mean we should not be diligent in shaving. Ledgers are much the same."

Elsa looked terribly troubled, as though she wasn't sure if she should laugh or not, but the bishop smiled gleefully.

"If you would please, then, Mister Lawrence."

"Of course. I can't guarantee I will have a plan for you, but I am willing to help if you're happy with what wisdom I can offer. I feel like this may be a problem that a money order could solve."

"Ohh!"

A broad smile crossed the bishop's face, and Sulto stood with wide eyes.

"Oh, I'm just musing aloud here. It's not like I've come up with a way to fix this yet," Lawrence hurriedly said as a disclaimer in response to their delight.

He had to make sure there was no direct line between the village and the church while still being honest about where the money was going.

There were several things a merchant could do at a time like this, but they would take a little work.

"Oh yes, of course. But you are *Lawrence*! The one who magicked all the debt away in town! I believe you will be able to come up with something for us, too."

The bishop's flattery brought a smile to Lawrence's face.

"We must inform the rest of the villagers right away. They must be beside themselves with nerves," Sulto said, rounding the table to firmly grasp both of Lawrence's hands and bow to Holo.

But unease suddenly came over Lawrence as he watched the mayor. Though he had said he would take on the job, he had a feeling he was missing something.

He was not nervous about how the money would get lent—nothing as technical as that. It was as though he was missing something even more fundamental…

Though the thoughts churned in his head, he could not think of anything. With a nettled feeling in his chest, he watched as Sulto moved to exit the room.

It happened as he placed his hand on the door.

"Hmm?" Holo hummed. A moment later, they heard excited voices coming from the hallway.

Sulto curiously pressed his ear to the door and glanced back at Lawrence and Holo.

But it seemed he knew what was going on.

"The villagers sound excited. I should go quiet them right awa—"

He only managed to say that much.

"Wait!"

"Please wait!"

They heard shouting from the hall.

"Please wait, Lord Rahden!"

Lawrence's eyes widened just as the door flung open.

"Lord Rahden?!"

Sulto was the first to speak up, and it was then that Lawrence realized what he had overlooked. He had come to learn of how the village in the Rahden Bishopric came to be, how it was faring in the present moment, Sulto and the other villagers' motives, and their passionate feelings for Rahden.

But there was one thing that never came up.

And that was what Rahden himself thought.

"Sulto! Why did you leave me behind in the village?!"

His voice was as loud as a mountain bear; he was no old hermit who spent his days in contemplation and prayer. Though his clothes resembled those of a monk, his head was shaved, and his wrinkles were so deep they seemed to be carved into his skin; he was so stout that he looked like a towering tree that had grown legs and started walking. His thick hands, the kind that were only found on those who toiled hard for years on end, were a testament to how tirelessly he had worked.

Rahden seemed much less like a fervent clergyman and more like a dutiful artisan who prioritized human feelings and relationships.

The man had complicated emotions coloring his face—ones that made him seem desperate to scream, but also desperate to cry—as he untangled himself from the villagers who tried to stop him.

"Lord Rahden! Why are you—?"

As Sulto began to speak, a young boy peeked out from beside the furious Rahden.

"Granddad! You can't hold talks without Lord Rahden!"

"Baum! Did you bring him here?!"

"I thought it was weird that you told me to go pick mushrooms with Lord Rahden. We took your horse."

Lawrence had completely forgotten to ask what Rahden thought of them borrowing money to give him peace of mind.

But the answer to that question was rather obvious.

"I understand you are the mayor, Sulto, but you were specifically instructed *not* to ask!"

"B-but, Lord Rahden! We were simply thinking of you and—"

"No, I've had enough of your impertinent talk! We are going back to the village, Sulto! The fishes are waiting for us!"

"Lord Rahden, please, listen! We came here because we are concerned for you and the village!"

The villagers tried to push Rahden back, but one twist of the waist and one grab of the arm had a grown man pulled into the air and tossed around like a cat.

Sulto was on the verge of tears; the boy, Baum, had raised his flag of rebellion against Sulto and the other villagers and brought Rahden to Salonia to fight alongside him.

The smooth-talking bishop was bewildered, and Holo was smiling in amusement at the sudden commotion.

What is going on? Lawrence sighed.

"Stop this at once!"

Hands slammed onto the table with a loud bang.

Everyone turned to look at Elsa—her brows knitted upward in rage.

"This is a church! A house of God! Under no circumstances will you cause a commotion in here!"

Her power was enough to make her fringe shudder; it surely came from constantly scolding three boys and a husband at home.

Rahden's, Sulto's and of course Baum's eyes widened. All the villagers reacted the same.

"Do you not understand that God is always watching?! Have you no shame?!"

Her reprimand was like a lash of a whip, and all the men drew up their shoulders at once.

The only sound in the quiet hall was Holo cackling quietly.

"Father, please show Mayor Sulto and the rest of the villagers to another room."

Sulto was about to protest, but when Elsa planted her hands on her hips and narrowed her eyes at him, he shrunk down like a little boy.

"Lord Rahden, and...young Baum. Stay here with me."

Rahden and Baum were certainly far enough apart to be grandfather and grandson, but the way they exchanged glances made them seem like friends.

"Come on! The rest of you, get to work!"

Elsa's command spurred the people into motion like a herd of sheep.

Sulto looked back at Rahden with regret, and though Rahden realized what was going on, he made no move to meet the man's gaze.

The manner in which Elsa brought the drink and poured some for everyone made it clear that she had hurt her throat raising her voice that way.

Rahden struggled to squeeze his large frame into a chair and remained silent as he peered into his cup.

"My name is Kraft Lawrence," Lawrence first introduced himself.

And as he thought, Rahden, being the frank man he was, lifted his head.

"...Rahden."

His reply was brief.

"That's an unusual name. Is it your family name, or…?"

"Lord Rahden's just Lord Rahden," the boy Baum interjected. "My name's Baum. Sulto's my granddad."

Holo took a liking to the fearless Baum in the blink of an eye. She smiled with delight when he turned to Elsa and asked, "Don't I get any wine?" and Elsa scolded him.

"So, Mister Lawrence, are you on my granddad's side?"

The boy got straight to the point.

Though he was the mayor's grandson, he was going against his will.

"I'm on no one's side right now."

"But weren't you cozying up with the church and going to do exactly what my granddad said just now?"

"I was going to, only because he asked, but this situation seems a little more complicated than that. I want to hear what you two have to say. That's why we had Mayor Sulto and the others leave."

Baum stared hard at Lawrence before scoffing and looking away.

"Was the mayor trying to borrow money from the church?" Rahden finally asked, and Lawrence nodded in response.

"Was this not a unanimous decision in the village?"

"…"

Rahden fell silent, and Baum spoke up instead.

"Everyone besides Lord Rahden and people like me who are on Lord Rahden's side agreed with borrowing money."

Lawrence got a general sense of where things stood in the village.

"Granddad said he was coming to do business in town, but he sent me and Lord Rahden off into the mountains, and I thought that was fishy. And just as I thought, when we got back, we heard that most of the villagers had come to town."

35

"That's why you rushed here on horseback?"

"Exactly. Lord Rahden can't ride a horse alone, you see."

The image of Baum taking the reins and Rahden sitting behind him was a rather strange one, but it brought a slight smile to Lawrence's face.

"Please pretend all this talk about a loan never happened," Rahden said. "The village has never needed a loan. It will not need any in the future."

"But Sulto said that you expressed some worries about the village's prospects in the future. He wants to borrow money to ease your worries."

"…"

Rahden fell silent.

"Are you worried because the hatchery isn't doing so well?"

Rahden made no motion to confirm or deny Lawrence's question, only stared into his cup.

"I think the hatchery didn't succeed because of the tanning," Baum interjected, his voice scarcely containing his annoyance. "We just need to stop tanning hides. Then we can let fish into the pond. Village goes back to normal."

There was no doubt that the tanning process could pollute the water. Lawrence glanced over at Holo because he thought investigating whether or not the tanning process was the cause was an option.

But Rahden turned to look at Baum and said, "The tanning has nothing to do with this. The water sources are clearly separated."

"But—"

Baum was about to argue, but Rahden's look was enough for him to keep quiet.

"I am worried," Rahden turned to look back at Lawrence. "The deer hunting is…not sustainable. I want to reestablish the hatchery in the village."

36

His unaffected language made him sound like a tree spirit. But a being who was one with nature currently sitting beside Lawrence seemed to twitch her ears ever so slightly under her hood.

"And I am not suited to becoming a bishop."

"Are you sure about that?" It was Elsa who spoke this time. "From what I have heard, you are more like a bishop than a great many who already wear the robes of one."

She sounded like she was stating an obvious fact—black was black, white was white—and it was oddly convincing.

Rahden was about to say something, but he eventually decided not to.

Elsa seemed slightly annoyed with him for a moment before continuing, "I have often been asked to manage the ledgers in churches across the area. Every bishop in every church I've visited has an impressive work history, but none have devoted themselves to studying the scripture, and they are all careless with money. I have always thought that such people need to be removed and replaced with bishops who are truly faithful."

Elsa's words caused Rahden to close his eyes with a wry smile.

"I know you are staunchly faithful," he said. "To hear that from you is a relief. It tells me that I have lived my life the way I should."

Though appearances made him seem as though he approached every problem with brute strength, his word choice made him sound like a genuine bishop.

"I am simply being honest," Elsa said.

Rahden's eyes snapped open and he turned to Baum, almost as though he was trying to avoid the problem.

"Everyone is overestimating me."

"Lord Rahden…"

There was a hint of frustration in Baum's voice, and Rahden sighed.

"Sir Lawrence, was it? My name is Rahden. Just Rahden. I left

37

my hometown when I was young, around Baum's age. It's been about forty years now. All those who knew my real name have likely departed this world by now."

Years of hard labor outside had left their mark on his skin—giving it a particular leathery quality created by the tanning process that was sweat, dust, and the sun. Rahden's bald head and hands were the same; he looked down at his hands as he continued.

"My home is the poor village of Rahdelli. You've heard of it, haven't you?"

Lawrence found himself unconsciously holding his breath when Rahden mentioned the place.

"I have, yes, but…are you really from that far away?"

Holo turned to look up at Lawrence, her head tilted.

"Um, you remember what I told you before, right? About the nobles who drizzle honey and lemon over ice? The land of eternal summer, of the burning desert? That's Rahdelli."

"Ha-ha, I do remember that myth."

In order to reach Rahdelli from Salonia, one had to head west and then take a boat from there.

It was entirely possible to travel partway on foot, but crossing the steep mountain range that blocked the way made it a life-threatening journey.

In one way or another, it would take at least three months to get there—six, in a worst-case scenario.

One would have to go to the southernmost point of the continent, and then once one encountered the warm, glittering seas there, one would have to take a boat across several islands to reach the opposite coast.

It was so far that Lawrence had only ever heard of its name.

"Rahdelli… Is that why you're named Rahden?"

Lawrence was certain that no one would ever find anyone else from Rahdelli in this area. There was no way Rahden would ever

38

find someone who would know his real name, which is why he had taken on the name of his homeland.

He understood that mindset after living on the road for so long.

"My village was run-down, dying. And the warm seas were full of sharks, so we could never catch enough fish. We…well, I'm not sure how you'd say it up here, but we made our living by searching for treasures in the sea. We rarely found any; maybe once a year. We were like pirates."

Treasures that could be found in the sea were typically amber that washed up on the beach after a storm, but when Rahden said they were pirates, Lawrence wondered if he commanded a famous group or something.

"After three years with no harvest, my village fell apart. I was all alone by that point, so I felt drawn by the land across the sea and wanted to see what was beyond. I got onto a trading vessel as a rower. I was strong enough after searching for sea jewels, so they put me to good use."

Rowing a ship was hard labor often used as punishment. That must have been what gave Rahden his physique.

"I went from ship to ship and eventually found myself in a cold land. The war between the Church and the northern pagans was at its peak then, and every boat had fervent clergy aboard. That was when I learned of God's teachings."

"Is that when you came to the area?" Lawrence asked.

"Hmm? Oh, yes. My master…I suppose you could call him that— I stuck right by his side and made my way to the site of the battle. But things were in a horrible state back then, and I couldn't move past this place. I couldn't abandon all the people I saw fleeing the very place we were headed for."

Rahden himself had left a destroyed village, so perhaps he found it even more difficult to leave them.

"When I left my master's side, he secured me all the privileges for the land where the village currently sits as a parting gift. He was charismatic enough to convert a bird with his sermons, so I suppose it was easy for him."

Realizing that it was not Rahden who had obtained the land originally brought Lawrence some relief.

"I decided I was going to live out my days here. I decided I was going to make this a home for people who had lost their own homes. I vowed to give my all to this place, so I dug up a puddle that had been filled with leaves and built a pond."

"Why a pond?"

Holo asked, almost in spite of herself.

Lawrence agreed. He also wanted to know why he had decided to build a fish hatchery.

A bashful look crossed Rahden's face.

"Because of the first passage I memorized from the scripture. God brought one loaf of bread and one fish to a starving people. The people ripped the loaf in two and gave one half to their neighbor, and someone else ripped their fish in two and gave one half to their neighbor. And so, one loaf of bread and one fish staved off hunger for a thousand people."

The bread-and-fish story was an allegory for loving one's neighbor, and Rahden had very nearly taken a literal interpretation of the tale.

"One after the other, people who had escaped the fires of war drifted here, and eventually the later arrivals who came because they had heard the rumors. Even women and children could care for the fish and help expand the pond. Everyone worked together, and we harvested loads of fish every year—more than I could have ever imagined as a child."

"Our trout is really good! Did either of you try it?"

When Baum asked, Lawrence shook his head.

"This is our first year here. We were so disappointed when we heard we couldn't have any."

"Oh..."

Baum was genuinely upset. Rahden smiled at him and continued his story.

"It was one thing after another, and forty years passed in the blink of an eye. So much time has passed—Sulto had been burned out of his home and arrived with a newborn in his arms; that newborn grew up and had his own child, who's already gotten this big."

Baum's lip curled in embarrassment under Rahden's tender gaze.

"I have followed God's teachings all my life. But I have no intentions of becoming a bishop. I will protect my village, and I will die in my village. That's all I pray for." Rahden's gaze lifted up to the ceiling, as though peering up to the heavens. "I wish to be buried by the pond, for plump trout to gather in the shade of the tree that will grow from my corpse. That is how I wish the village to be." He lowered his gaze and said quietly, "That is all I want."

There was strength in his voice despite his age, but that only served to season the tones of sadness of a man in his elder years.

Holo's head was drooped, her hands balled into fists in her lap. Though aloof she seemed, she had the kindest heart, and these kinds of stories affected her more than anyone else Lawrence knew.

"Even if the church here lent the villagers enough money to never have to work another day in their lives?" Lawrence asked, almost jokingly, and Rahden only gave him a tired smile.

"I will not go to the pope. I have no reason to leave the village."

Lawrence thought he saw Holo's ears twitch beneath her hood, but she was likely more affected by the wish Rahden ultimately confessed to them.

Lawrence glanced at Holo before saying, "All right."

Rahden studied Lawrence for a moment before silently bowing his head.

The people of the Rahden Bishopric had come to town without arranging for a place to stay ahead of time, so the bishop decided that they would be allowed to stay the night at the church. Lawrence wanted to say it was a fitting decision coming from the church, the embodiment of God's mercy, but the bishop did not seem to be the type to sweat the details—he had likely made the decision on the fly. Elsa, who would likely be charged with keeping them under control due to her peerless work ethic, was weary.

"Things have taken an odd turn..."

When she had come to see Lawrence and Holo off, her words then had also been heavy with exhaustion.

"I'd say this is much better than uncovering the problem after talks have progressed."

There was the stubborn Rahden, and then Sulto and the people of the village, who respected Rahden so much that they would act rashly on his behalf even if it meant going against his wishes.

This was not a logical matter, which meant there was no correct approach to the problem; Lawrence only hoped that they could settle this in a way where they could fondly look back on this in several years' time and laugh.

"I'll come again tomorrow."

"Thank you. I will keep watch to make sure the Father doesn't bring out any ale."

The bishop was not a bad person, but it was clear that he was not a very attentive clergyman, especially since he had thrown a merchant in prison simply because he felt it was something he should do during the whole kerfuffle over debts.

"Good night, then."

"Good night," Elsa said, tired, and went back into the church, her shoulders slightly hunched over.

Once the moment had gone, Lawrence turned to Holo beside him.

"You're going to be up for a little while after we get back to the inn, right?"

After choosing the whisky that would be used in the festival the night before, Holo had drunk herself silly in a drinking contest.

She did not wake up at any point in the morning, of course, and was still in poor spirits during the day; it was only when the sun began to set that she went back to normal. All she had eaten that day were sardines and a bit of soup for a snack. That, and the town was at its liveliest, what with the end of the market overlapping with the festival preparations.

The hustle and bustle of town in the late hour was even greater than it had been during the day, and most of the revelers were inebriated.

"Aye. I desire fatty meat."

"Okay, okay."

They entered a nearby tavern at her insistence.

Lawrence sipped his ale as he watched Holo sink her teeth into a lamb chop.

The great market was where all the agricultural products came together, so it was not just the town distillers who were showing off their wares—there were also those who used their own stills and secret techniques. What Lawrence was drinking was

43

made of barley smoked in wood hewn from fruit trees, imparting a fruity flavor.

It was easy to drink; he had a feeling Holo could down an entire barrel if left to her own devices.

"Whose side do you think we should take?"

"Mm?"

After washing down the greasy mutton with her own ale, Holo turned to Lawrence, a thick foam mustache adorning her lip.

"I'd normally approach this like a merchant and weigh things on the scale, if it were a matter of logic."

There was a lot of emotion involved in this disagreement between Sulto and Rahden.

"Or maybe I shouldn't get involved at all?"

An outsider meddling in these affairs usually made things worse.

The debt plaguing the town just happened to be an issue that was easier for an outsider to solve.

That said, this particular problem did not seem as steep a hurdle, but neither was it one that they could solve themselves.

"For what reason would you want to help them?"

Holo took the clean lamb bone in hand and frantically waved down the tavern girl who was carrying around food.

"Because it'd be a waste if I didn't."

"Would it?"

Holo, biting into the roasted beans that had come with her lamb, looked at him with surprise.

"A merchant you've never seen before is selling really high-quality mutton in the market. But he doesn't realize the quality of the meat himself, so he's trying to sell it off cheaply to people who cook meat together in a hodgepodge at their cheap stalls."

"What a fool! Good mutton has an herbal scent to it, and is best cooked in a bread oven or something of the sort. Meat scraps taste best boiled!"

44

"See? You'd want to speak up, wouldn't you?"

Holo nodded.

"Do you mean to say this is no different?"

"Exactly. He's reclaimed land obtained through dubious means and built such a wonderful little village. People have taken to calling him a bishop, but he's not a man of the clergy at all. One day, however, an invitation to actually become one comes directly from the pope, and he turns that down for some reason?"

A bishop was a very high position in the clergy. It was typically a title only obtained after deep study of theology of one's own will, mastering high-level canon law while serving at a church, then taking a slow journey up the Church's ladder starting as assistant priest.

It was not attainable through faith alone; one needed cunning and political chops and to give plenty of gratuities to senior clergy in order to cross these barriers.

But to be given the opportunity to skip all of that and immediately become a bishop, only to turn the position down? Anyone would call that a waste.

"Perhaps he simply isn't interested. Little Col loves the scripture, but he is not the type to swagger about a church, no?"

"I have a feeling this is a bit more than just plain old interest. If he were to become a bishop, then his village would become the formal seat of a diocese. There is real benefit to that happening, and anyone who is genuinely concerned for the village's well-being should be able to see that."

"Mm."

Holo gave a halfhearted response; either she was not sure what Lawrence was getting at, or it was because she had just seen them take out a hunk of mutton from the oven in the kitchen.

"The bishop here said the same thing, but the Rahden Bishopric has rights to the land on behalf of a church that doesn't exist.

If a descendant of the former noble owner or anyone like that came in claiming the whole thing was a scam, then there would be nothing they could do to fight it."

"I…suppose that could happen, yes."

"But if a real bishop were in charge of the bishopric, then the Church would side with them in a tough situation like that. The noble would have to *really* fight if they wanted the land back in that case. It'd be the same as fighting with any other landowner."

Just as Lawrence finished speaking, the sprightly tavern girl, her red hair tied back with a ribbon, set the plate of freshly grilled mutton on their table.

Holo asked for seconds of her drink as the tavern girl passed by before taking her knife and carving a line in the meat.

"All this is mine."

She was putting territorial dispute into practice.

"And if the town falls into financial trouble in the future, then it would be much easier for the Salonia church to lend a hand. People rarely question when money passes between churches, nor do they think it very problematic."

"I understand that. Back when I was naught but your traveling companion, 'twas quite painful to simply have a meal because you would always be paying. You should know how much it eases my consciousness now that I am your wife."

"…"

Lawrence turned to her wordlessly, his lips drawn in a strained smile, and in turn she gave him a sweet-yet-sinister smile in return. She then cut into the meat with joy and bit into it.

"Well, if Rahden does become bishop, that title comes with all kinds of perks, you see. Even if the worst of the worst happens to the village, he wouldn't need to worry nearly as much."

After crunching her way through the cartilage, Holo spoke

without bothering to wipe her mouth. "There must be disadvantages, too, no?"

Of course that was where her mind would go. She was the wisewolf.

"Of course. He'd be a part of the Church, so whoever assumes his position would be in a position higher than the mayor."

"Mm. I can imagine this would be a particular handful of an individual."

"I think that might be what Rahden's worried about."

Rahden had nurtured and developed the village up under his own personal care. He would not be very happy if an outsider came in and started acting like it was their own.

As those thoughts crossed Lawrence's mind, he took a piece of mutton, smaller than the smallest portion Holo had cut for him, and bit into it. The sweet fats filled his mouth.

"And you noticed something while Rahden was talking, didn't you?" Lawrence asked. Holo, who was hunched over as she munched into her mutton ribs, lifted her gaze at him with rounded eyes.

"'Twas nothing notable. He said deer hunting was unstable, so he was hoping to bring the hatchery back to the village, no?"

"Was he lying?"

Holo shrugged her slender shoulders; she stared fixedly at the stripped bone, then sunk her canines into a sinewy piece of meat that still clung to it.

"You said that his deer hunting was going well. Perhaps the fool simply dislikes the thought of it."

The way she spoke made it sound like she was deliberately putting emotional distance between her and him. Lawrence sensed that she was not keen on touching the heart of the issue, though it did not seem to be major enough to consider her to be hiding something.

As he wondered why that was, he recalled what Rahden had said.

"Maybe Rahden built the lake in the mountains not to get rich, but because he was sentimental about the home he left behind."

The man had said that the first passage he learned from the scripture had guided him to do so, but it was still rather unnatural to build a lake, of all things.

Holo did not respond right away; after munching on her bone with loud crunching noises, she placed it down with a sigh.

"I know not how people think."

Her remark sounded heartless, but Lawrence knew how she felt deep inside.

She once lived in a place called Yoitsu with her friends, and she left one day on a total whim. Though she had intended to return straightaway, at the end of her wanderings she found herself overseeing the wheat harvest in a town called Pasloe by strange coincidence. She claimed she had made a promise with a villager she met there and ended up fulfilling that role for centuries out of a sense of obligation. Time passed, Holo forgot the way home, and her old friends were lost to the ravages of time. There was no one left to answer her lonesome howls.

And despite all that, Lawrence had brought up the topic of re-creating a lost home.

A problem that was typically kept buried, one that was unsolvable, showed its face at times like this.

Though he understood why she would want to distance herself from the concept, there was still one thing he did not understand.

"But that doesn't really have anything to do with becoming a bishop."

So what did that mean?

Lawrence sat thinking, mug of ale in hand, but his thoughts

didn't lead him to a clear conclusion. In all honesty, it seemed preposterous that Rahden would turn down the position of bishop. He also could not find a sensible reason for him to be so harsh on the busybody Sulto, or for it to turn into the big scuffle it did at the church.

There had to be another reason why Rahden would refuse the position.

As those thoughts ruminated in his mind, he noticed Holo was looking at him from across the mutton with a weary look on her face.

"Hmm? Wh-what is it? What's wrong?"

He brought his hand up to his face in surprise, wondering if something was stuck to him, then looked down at the mutton, also wondering if he had accidentally cut a piece of the fatty part for himself, which was Holo's favorite bit.

When she saw his reaction, she sighed.

After a moment of heavy hesitation, she opened her mouth.

"Dear, I think—"

Just as she was about to continue, a loud voice cut her off.

"Well, well! If it isn't Sir Lawrence!"

They looked up in surprise to see a man with a bald head, full beard, and round belly—Laud, the very picture of an elderly merchant. He was the owner of the company that first presented his loan bonds to them when Salonia was in an uproar over debts.

Ever since then, he had come to see Lawrence as the hero of mercantilism.

"Your wife is beautiful, as always."

Though Holo typically was the kind to readily accept compliments like that, she only offered a vague smile in return, having been interrupted just as she was about to say something.

"You know, I heard that the church was swarmed by folk from the Rahden Bishopric, and that they called for you specifically,

49

Sir Lawrence. That was about whether Lord Rahden is going to be a real bishop, wasn't it?"

Everyone knew at this point since Sulto had discussed the matter with many trading companies.

"Yes… They say that the merchants in town turned down their requests for loans."

Lawrence's tone was teasing because he knew that Laud was one of the ones who had turned them down. Laud himself shrugged, mug filled to the brim with ale in one hand, at the implication.

"We wouldn't have minded a small loan…but they asked for quite a bit, and you know how things have been. And if Lord Rahden was to become a real bishop, then the problems would start once someone comes to take his place. There is more than a small chance of us never getting repaid."

Lawrence had considered that very issue; any merchant could think of at least one or two real-life examples of such a thing happening.

"But my business partners and I agree that it would be a good thing if it were to become a real bishopric. When I saw you, I had to find out what you think."

"I don't think this will be quite what you're expecting, but…"

Laud took a sip of his drink and gave a sympathetic smile. "Lord Rahden himself doesn't sound too enthused about the idea, does he?"

It sounded as though he knew that already.

"Why do you think that is?" Lawrence asked.

The outer edges of Laud's eyes, red from the alcohol, drooped as he replied, "Hmm… You know, I find that strange, too. Speaking logically, being made bishop is like being a country girl that a prince wants to marry. I know it'd be a lot of work, but if someone's inviting you to take the throne, you'd take it, wouldn't you?"

Lawrence laughed in spite of himself, but the metaphor was indeed accurate.

"Well, he'd have to leave the village for a while if he became bishop. I bet it's because that hatchery of his isn't going so well. The mayor and all of them are busy with deer hunting and all those products, so Lord Rahden must think he's the only one who can do it."

When Lawrence had asked if Sulto was going to revive the hatchery with the loan, the mayor had given an evasive answer.

He must have thought that putting money and effort into a difficult-to-maintain hatchery while the deer business was going well was not the best course of action.

"And Lord Rahden set up that whole pond because he wanted to re-create the ideal seas from his hometown, didn't he?"

"So that *is* the reason why, isn't it?"

It had been nothing more than their own speculation before this conversation, so Lawrence latched on to what Laud said.

"Obviously. Better if there was a nice pond out there to begin with, but he went through all the trouble to dig a hole and fill it with water. Tugs at the heartstrings, doesn't it? The mayor and his friends should help him out, I say, even if it doesn't make them a fortune." Laud sounded disappointed. "All that fatty fish was so tasty, too," he murmured; that was likely how he genuinely felt.

But something about the pond and Rahden re-creating his ideal hometown did not quite add up in Lawrence's mind.

"But didn't his dreams come true already?"

"Hmm?" Laud hummed in reply.

"I hear it's written in Salonia's annals—the fish were so abundant one year that it saved Salonia from famine."

"Oh, yes, that was back when I was a snot-nosed brat. I remember. It was the tastiest trout in all the world."

Which then begged the question: Why was Rahden still so attached to it?

51

"By the way, the mayor and the others didn't say anything about filling up the lake, did they?"

It was a worry of all men who worked away from home that something would happen to their secret savings while they were gone.

When Laud heard the possibility, he howled with laughter.

"Ha! Who'd be so stupid? If the bishop were to give up on the hatchery, then they'd use that water for tanning, anyway! I'd say the mayor and his friends would only deepen their faith in it, thinking since Lord Rahden made it, it might even be a miracle spring that could save them twice!"

When he put it that way, he was likely right. Though it was not the same picturesque ocean from the man's hometown, it was still put to good use for the villagers.

Rahden would be gone for just one year to get the formalities done that would make him a bishop. And judging by the way Laud spoke about it, it was hard to imagine Sulto and the others turning the pond into a tanning workshop while Rahden was away.

In that case, Rahden should be fully able to return from becoming a bishop and get back to reestablishing the hatchery.

As Lawrence hummed in thought, Laud suddenly thrust his face toward Lawrence's, a teasing remark accompanied by breath that stunk of alcohol.

"The lads and I think that Lord Rahden might be close to realizing a second dream of his."

"What?"

"They used to search for gems at the bottom of the sea back in his hometown, didn't they?"

"Or so I've heard, yes… What?! Wait, but how—"

Lawrence honestly wondered how they were supposed to find treasure from a hole in a mountain that they built, and Laud's shoulders shook with laughter.

"Ha-ha-ha! That's just tavern banter! But it *is* hard to see how any of it makes sense without something like that, you know."

"Yes, it is puzzling."

"Heh. People have come to talk to the other merchants in town about the very same thing. Everyone comes to the same conclusion. But everyone says that it'll be different because you're around this time."

Lawrence understood now.

"We're all betting on how this'll end, you know."

Laud had come to gather information from him so that he would have an advantage on his bet.

He winked mischievously.

"I wonder what that treasure could be. Sadly, I can't seem to figure it out," Lawrence mused.

"Hmm?"

"Up in the northern seas, you can find amber washed ashore after a storm. Or...pearls, perhaps?"

While large chunks of amber were hard to come by, one could almost always collect smaller pieces. Pearls were rarer, but they were a by-product of shellfish, so it did not make too much sense that a village would perish without harvesting them for three whole years. It made sense if they were unable to produce or catch any shells, but that did not seem to be the case.

"It won't be amber or pearls," Laud said. "What did he say...? It's not something you hear about too much up here. It was, uh..." He patted his smooth head, and his eyes widened in an instant. "That's right! Coral!"

"Coral?"

"Long ago, I saw a traveling handicraft merchant present a sample of their wares to a noble. It was beautiful, red and gemlike. It had silver filigree on it, so it was rounded, but I hear it used to be like a tree that grows in the sea."

53

A tree that grew in the sea—though Lawrence had only heard about it in passing once, that was precisely the impression he had of it.

He couldn't form a clear mental image of it, but it did make sense that out of all the things in this wide, wide world, a tree of gems could grow in the sea.

"They grow at the bottom of the ocean, and it's hard to get down there and harvest them. That's why they make hooks to attach to metal rods that look like the Church crest, wrap rope around them, and drop them into the water. They pull the hooks up again, then dunk them back in. The whole job's based on luck—it's absolutely disheartening. And those trunks have to be thick enough in order to carve jewels out of them, which makes the whole ordeal even more luck-based."

"I see…" Lawrence was impressed; there was still so much about the world he did not know. He gave Laud a tired smile. "I highly doubt they could re-create that in a pond, though."

"But dreams are dreams, right?"

Laud was right.

"Well, guess we still don't know. Lord Rahden won't give his reasoning based on anything but the hatchery."

That told Lawrence that going to ask the man himself would not give him an answer.

"Either way, if it looks like Lord Rahden might become a bishop, just let me know. I'd want to donate something to him as a symbol of our acquaintanceship."

Laud gave a businesslike smile and returned to his own seat.

Lawrence was relieved that the man's large and overbearing presence was gone, but the emptiness in his chest almost felt like everything had been in vain.

"Hmm… Now I'm even more confused than before," Lawrence murmured with a sigh, folding his arms.

They could not force Rahden into becoming a bishop if he himself was not interested, but from the outside, it seemed like a total waste if he did not take the opportunity. Both Lawrence and Laud, of course, were secretly invested in this situation, because it would mean another ally in the Church for them.

And Lawrence also felt a sense of understanding to how forceful Sulto's actions seemed in contrast to Rahden's motives.

Sulto and the other villagers were genuinely thankful for all Rahden had done for them. They likely saw this as their chance to repay their debts to him.

Rahden, especially, had apparently traveled all this way with the Church's teachings serving as the wind in his sails. It would make sense if he wanted to become a real member of the clergy, and would think that this was his God-given chance.

But in fact, seeing an elderly individual who had led people all their lives, plus all the people around them who greatly respected said individual, was a common sight in the Nyohhira baths.

There could be two generations of nobility who come to the baths. The father is so old that he no longer has any teeth, yet he still insists that he can keep up with the youths. His son might be old enough to have pronounced wrinkles on his face, yet he grumbles about how his father keeps patrolling their land on horseback and keeps participating in complicated manorial affairs that last well into the night for days in a row.

The father will never listen, no matter how much the son insists he rest, so the son drags his father all the way out to Nyohhira in order to get him to slow down for a moment.

It is only then that the father realizes it is time to retire.

"I bet Rahden knows, logically, that he should become a bishop, but..." Lawrence muttered, but he realized at the same time that Holo, sitting across from him, had her head drooped, staring down into her mug. "Hey, are you okay?"

She had been quiet ever since Laud came by, but she looked pale as well. Though her cheeks were reddened, she seemed abnormally pallid besides that. She'd only had two or three mugs of ale, this was right after a hangover, so perhaps it was having an adverse effect on her.

There was still a bit of mutton left, too—a sure sign that she was not well. It seemed as though their best option was to wrap the food up and take it back to the inn.

"Let's go back, Holo."

He plucked the mug of ale from her hand as she drowsily nodded off, paid the bill to the redheaded tavern girl, hoisted Holo onto his back, and took the pack of mutton.

Exasperated, he wondered how many times he had carried her back to their inn so far, but she likely had her guard down because she knew he would do this for her.

He did sometimes wonder if it was an act, but he, of course, always pretended not to notice.

It was a merchant's pleasure to meet the demands of the customer.

If his princess was going to beg for attention, then he was going to spoil her rotten.

"Sure is chilly."

When they left the tavern, the air was heavy with signs of autumn. He wondered if he should have placed a blanket over Holo, but he grimaced at the thought—that would be a bit too much.

He readjusted her on his back as she seemed about to slip off, and slowly headed back toward their inn.

"I feel like she's getting heavier every year..."

He thought it strange, considering how her appearance never changed, but then it dawned on him that she was not the one changing. Holo was not getting heavier; Lawrence was the one withering away.

One day, him carrying Holo on his back to bed would become a distant memory of the past.

He wondered if the reason why he was so quick to answer her demands was because he would always imagine things from her perspective.

Only Holo would stay young forever; only Lawrence would grow old with age. Whenever he pictured the day he would leave Holo behind in this world, he found himself desperate to indulge her. Sometimes, he felt like it would never be enough.

He could not protect her forever. They had vowed in their marriage to stay together "till death do us part," and they had always known that Lawrence would be the first to go.

Lawrence forced a smile as the customers gathered around the bar outside the inn hooted at them. The innkeeper silently stepped ahead of him to open the door for him and prepared a small bucket for them just in case.

As Lawrence, tired, was about to place Holo on the bed, she stirred awake.

She stretched out her legs to get down and sat on the bed with a forceful *thud*.

"This is starting to feel familiar." Lawrence smiled.

Holo curled up and groaned.

"You feeling okay?"

There was more color in her face now, but when he asked her, just in case, she nodded. Of course, he did not trust her, since she did not loudly claim she was handling it fine, but she did more than just nod.

She reached out to grab his sleeve in a gesture for him to sit beside her.

"I'm coming, I'm coming."

Holo looked much younger when she was weak. They often said that a person became more childish the older they became. He sat on her right side, and she placed her forehead on his shoulder.

"I apologize, I cannot hold my liquor…"

She was telling him what was wrong, which meant she was feeling much better.

Lawrence wrapped his arm around Holo and grasped her hand with his own free one.

"Laud did drop by in the middle of our conversation. Bet you felt lonely, huh?" he teased her, and she gripped his hand even tighter. "I'm sorry," he said, and kissed the base of her ear.

She cared for her tail using expensive oils, which gave it a sweet floral scent. But there was a different sweetness to her ears—they smelled like her.

He restrained himself, though, because he knew she did not like it when he sniffed her too much, when she suddenly spoke up.

"Lonely is likely an apt descriptor."

"…"

In his shock, a pacifying smile reflexively crossed his face.

"No, I *was* lonely. And I am sorry for not being able to hold my liquor."

She rubbed the base of her ears against his cheek.

Up until that point, Lawrence had nothing to say in return to her shyness, but his thoughts finally caught up.

"…Oh, right. You were going to say something right as Laud came to us, weren't you?"

Had she realized something about Rahden? Now that he thought about it, she had been looking glum ever since then. He gently shook her hand, waiting for an answer, and her small hands shook back.

"All you do is think and think…and I realized that you are a fool."

"Hmm?"

He only hummed in response, and she dug her nails into his hand.

"You are a fool, despite how intelligent you are. Intelligent enough to surprise me. The answer has been right in front of you this whole time." It sounded as though she was speaking in riddles. "Or perhaps *I* am the fool," she continued. "After all, with my nose and ears being so sharp, I never realized my weakness was in my eyes."

The topic had come up in Nyohhira. The reason Holo had always been so bad with reading and writing was because her eyesight was poorer than she realized. When she took her first look through reading spectacles—polished glass that could magnify writing—she had been shocked.

What did that mean, then, on a larger scale?

Thoughts slowly churned through Lawrence's head, and he finally replied, "…I'm looking at it with too many preconceptions?"

Thinking logically, Rahden's actions did not make much sense. Being selected to be bishop was a miracle on the level of a prince falling in love with a peasant girl, yet he was keen to turn down the offer. And no matter how he looked at it, that would guarantee a stable foundation for the village for future generations.

If he valued the village above all else, then Lawrence felt that he should simply become a bishop for the greater good, even if it inconvenienced him in a way.

That meant what was keeping Rahden from doing so was not grounded in logic.

When it came to matters of logic, of trade, then Lawrence had plenty of opinions.

But he was no match for Holo when it came to sentimental matters, ones that dealt with human subtlety.

"I was thinking about that great tree of a man for the entire time."

Rahden was not a bear, not a stone, but a tree.

He was, indeed, a lot like a tree.

"Why does such a stubborn tree like him not acknowledge the concerns of those around him?"

That was where Holo's thoughts began. And that meant, at the very least, that Sulto's concern for Rahden was genuine.

And though they had approached the matter from the very same starting point, Holo had looked at it from an entirely different angle.

"I...was honestly irritated by this. He does not know how lucky he is."

Lawrence gasped in realization not because he did not know how Holo felt...

...but because he felt similarly to when he crossed a line he shouldn't have.

"Do you mean...?"

He trailed off, not finishing his sentence, and Holo smiled as she closed her eyes.

"Yes. Pasloe. I lived there for such a long time, no?" Her tone was sleepy, as though she was recounting an old tale. "Until I was chased away, that is."

Lawrence inhaled deeply and held his breath.

Though to him, Pasloe was where he and Holo met, to Holo, it was a village where she had lost something dear to her.

"I cared deeply for those people, and yet they were the ones who chased me away. To me, I find it absurd that this big tree was moaning and groaning over all the love and luck he has."

Though there was jest in her tone, he knew she was partially serious.

Her tail, laid out behind him, bristled.

"But his pain is real. He is hesitant, and it hurts him. He has put his life on the line to protect his people, and they in turn worry about him from the bottom of their hearts—so why? I wondered. It does not make sense. And that is why..." She sat up, lifting herself from Lawrence. "...I pictured myself in his stead. I pictured how the tree might feel."

"Rahden?"

Holo nodded, a strained smile crossing her face, as though someone had touched her leg after it had fallen asleep.

"This Rahden must think he is being chased out of his village, no?"

"Hmm? ...What? Chased out?" Lawrence asked in turn, not quite understanding what she meant.

"Perhaps...'chased out' is not the correct wording. But it is similar."

The concern of Sulto and the others was genuine, and Holo's sharp ears would have been able to discern whether or not they were secretly planning on ousting Rahden.

Lawrence looked at her quizzically, and she gave a tired smile.

"Think about it. Remember the hatchery pond? The thing he gave his all to build? All of those fish died."

"But...I'm pretty sure the villagers are genuinely thankful for everything he's done for them. They even found a living off the deer because they didn't want to burden him anymore, right?"

"Aye. Precisely. And if I were in his shoes..." Holo directed her gaze out the window to the night sky, then looked back at Lawrence, forcefully planting her face on his chest in a headbutt. "...I would be lonely."

"You…would?"

Holo nodded, not bothering to show him her face.

"Those in Pasloe, too, used human knowledge and power to devise ways to cultivate their wheat. Their wheat was bountiful without my help. I should not have minded if someone were to come up with a way to get bountiful harvests; they used to ask me to do that for them, after all. I should have been happy for them and their harvests."

"…"

Lawrence could tell from her voice that she was on the verge of tears, and that, in turn, pained him.

But he wanted to cry for a different reason.

That was because once he saw what she wanted to say, he felt a clear frustration with his own carelessness.

"'Tis the same with his pond. 'Twould not be surprising that one of his reasons lay in the dream of re-creating his home. But I believe his biggest reason for doing so was to fill the stomachs of the hungry." She sniffed and continued, her tone as though she were thinking back on a time when she served Pasloe as its protector as Holo the Wisewolf. "To bring smiles to his people. To give a new home to his new family. What he did to accomplish that should not have mattered. Logically, at least."

Though her head was still bowed, Lawrence could tell that she was clearly smiling when she said *logically*.

It was as though she was laughing at herself for being a fool for feeling hurt over what happened in Pasloe.

She had been lost to the sands of time in her life in Pasloe; on top of that, she had been deemed a symbol of a bad custom left-over from days gone by, and that had hurt her so much that her massive wolf form almost vanished completely.

She wanted to find her way home anyway, so she could have easily caused the village more trouble on her way out, but she had not been able to bring herself to do so.

Because it was not logical.

The bonds of obligation and duty were not so easily shed.

"It felt as though someone else existed inside me. That tree must feel the same way. He is a large man, and he seems smart. He must surely understand what that white-haired mayor says and feels. Yet he does not listen to his heart... That must be it."

It was not just Sulto, Baum, and the other villagers who both praised and worried about Rahden, but the bishop of Salonia and Elsa were much the same. The deer business began because the villagers had been worried that Rahden was working too much. Everyone was thinking of him.

But what was it like from *his* perspective?

You built a hatchery pond for the people of your village, but the fish died out, and now the villagers have found jobs they can accomplish on their own. You were the only one making any effort to revitalize the hatchery, and yet the villagers insist you spend a year far away from the village to become a bishop and not worry about them.

And so it would not be strange at all if this is how it sounded to Rahden:

Become a bishop. That is the only purpose you serve now.

That idea must have come to hang heavy over him, much in the way how inescapable the curtain of night always was.

"And I believe he has bad knees. He certainly could not join in hunting deer."

"What?"

Lawrence was genuinely surprised to hear that.

"What, had you not noticed?" Holo asked, lifting her head as she sniffed again. He shook his head, laying bare his foolery.

"But didn't he break free when the other villagers tried to pin him down?"

"He rooted himself with his left leg only. Perhaps that is why

63

he cannot ride a horse well; it is much too dangerous for him to mount and dismount."

She wiped at the corners of her eyes with her hands.

Lawrence pictured Rahden as he watched Holo, not entirely intending to look at her so intently. Even now, Rahden was large and powerful; he could easily imagine how overflowing with strength he had been in his youth.

Even Lawrence had felt such exhaustion carrying a drunk Holo on his back, which made him feel sad, and realize just how much he'd aged.

And so, for one who had cultivated such hardiness in one's body throughout their entire lives, it must have been an even greater shock.

As hurt knees kept him from working, he could do nothing but watch the fish in the hatchery die. Either it was his knees, or the restoration was not going as planned. Watching the villagers easily carry out hunting that he could not participate in would only make his state of mind much, much worse.

Now that Lawrence thought about it, Rahden seemed so miserable when asked to sit in his chair.

The reason he was so attached to the hatchery was not because of the sea from his hometown.

That was because he was desperately trying to keep all the water he had cupped in his hands from spilling.

He was trying to maintain his memory of a time when he served as the heart of the village, when he was the great tree that held up the sky above them.

Yet now his knees, which had previously held up his convictions, were giving out on him.

His body would only decline further. His purpose in the village would dwindle.

Rahden was being swallowed by the rapids of time and was drowning.

"'Tis frightening to lose one's place in the world."

Holo knew the dread of being left alone in this wide, wide world. She knew how harsh it was not to be needed anymore.

Lawrence looked at her—really looked at her.

He thought she had been crying, but she was smiling.

"I know I called you a fool for how much you go 'round and 'round with your logic." Holo sniffed again, a smile still on her face. "But I should have noticed right away back in the church, but I had been unable to. That is because…" She paused, a bashful tone overtaking her smile before continuing, "…you gave me a home. Your care and your love made me forget all the sad things the world had to offer. Because our place is overflowing with warm springs, and it is a comfortable place."

Her carefree smile only caused Lawrence's heart to ache even more.

He truly felt as though he had been doing so much for Holo.

But all the good deeds in the world could not assuage her loneliness forever.

He pulled her small frame into a tight embrace, the physical manifestation of a wish that time would stop in place for them.

And what came out of his mouth next…were spiteful remarks.

"*And* I feed you and give you alcohol, so you really don't have much to complain about."

"You fool! I have been so honest w—"

"And *that's* why…"

Lawrence somehow managed to subdue the unease in his chest, Holo still in his arms as she began to yell at him.

He slowly let her go and pinched her nose, an earnest, teasing smile on his face.

"That's why if I accept all of your feelings as they are, I'm going to want to give you literally everything, every last coin I have. Then you won't have any money left to drink by the next year, right?"

Holo's feelings were like a big barrel of wine. They needed small portions at a time; otherwise they would overindulge, get very drunk, and fall headfirst into the barrel.

"Miss Elsa just taught you the importance of family finance, didn't she?"

When he brought up her name, it was almost funny how deeply Holo's face twisted into a frown.

"And you've been drinking far too much these past few days anyway."

Holo finally pouted.

"I have not spent a single coin."

She was right—since they were the ones to have solved the town's financial problem, no matter what tavern they went to, they would be treated to some drink or another. That said, she was apparently aware that she had been drinking too much; she lifted her feet onto the bed, hugged her knees, and looked away in a huff.

Lawrence smiled with a sigh and said, "And I'm lonely when you're out drunk."

Holo's mouth fell open slightly in astonishment as she stared at Lawrence.

Then, as her stiff expression loosened, the corner of her mouth turned upward, as though she was trying desperately to keep her delight to herself.

"…You are a fool."

"And?"

"Look at you, this is why you—"

"—will always be a cute boy?"

He knew she was going to call him a fool, so he decided to finish her sentence for her.

She was vexed, having been beaten to the punch, yet she still smiled in delight.

"It isn't about logic," Lawrence said.

He was speaking about himself, but also about Rahden.

Sulto was the logical one here.

But Rahden was the one whose emotions could not be dealt with purely through logic alone.

"Aye. The problem lies in his anxieties. The tree is not a true tree."

It was the same as Holo—though her true form was a massive wolf, one big enough to swallow a man whole, that did not mean her heart was as steely and animalistic.

Leaving the two parties on separate pages would be like leaving Holo by herself in Pasloe.

"Then what should we do?" Lawrence asked, almost to himself, and Holo reached up to gingerly brush his cheek.

"You have seen what we should do at our bathhouse in Nyohhira."

"We have? Ah, you mean…when titles change hands between nobles."

She was talking about when two generations of nobles came to their bathhouse. He had always thought that those who clung to their power and refused to let go were always a handful.

But understanding better now that they were simply afraid of losing their place in the world, he felt like he could treat them with plenty of kindness.

"You typically start off by praising all their accomplishments in life, right? When it comes to the ritual in passing down headship."

"Give your thanks, but be careful not to give too much. It makes sense."

Though late into his career it was, he was learning something new. He had not thought too deeply about it when they were in Nyohhira.

"Then what has Rahden accomplished?"

It went without saying that he had built a pond in an empty mountainside, raised countless fish, and fed the hungry.

But if they were to express their true thanks, then they would have to bring up how he brought the entire village together and did all he could to reestablish the hatchery. It would have been nice if there were infinite resources and labor, but Sulto and the other villagers had finally found stability from work in the deer industry.

To abandon all that and return to the unstable hatchery business was too risky.

They needed to express their thanks with something else.

Something that could shine a light on all the time, money, and energy he had spent on them so far.

"That tree would scavenge for gems in the sea from his hometown, no? Myuri likes those bards' tales that end in a similar fashion?"

"Do you mean the ones that go like, *And the true gem to the villagers was the fish, and they all lived happily ever after*? Those ones?"

"...Hmm, it sounds rather cheap when you put it that way."

Lawrence hummed, then suddenly remembered that selected passages of the translated scripture were sitting on their desk.

"Oh, right, didn't Rahden say he memorized a passage from the scripture and dug out a pond in the mountains because of it?"

"The passage about the fish? 'Twould be better if it were about meat," Holo said, based purely on personal preference, but Lawrence reached out and grabbed the bundle of passages. This was not the entire scripture, only a collection of the most common

68

tales from it. This was the result of everything Col had done—studying every day, enduring drowsiness as he ate raw onions.

As he flipped through it, Lawrence found plenty of fables he knew, and the story about the fish was included, too. Similarly, he found other passages about food; they must be popular.

With the passages written in the vernacular, Lawrence was surprised at how easy they were to understand. He almost felt a fool for trying so hard to learn how to read the church's script.

As page after page went by, his heart was captured by a particular sentence that leaped out at him.

"Ah, yes, this gem of the sea is—Mm? What is the matter?"

Holo peered curiously at him.

With Lawrence's gaze at the booklet in his hands, Holo squinted at the writing on the page, and her tail puffed up not long after.

"Oh ho! I see!"

"What do you think?" Lawrence asked her, and Holo was shockingly happy about it.

"I was just thinking the same thing. 'Twas almost as though I had been waiting for you to find that sentence."

"Huh? What do you mean?"

There must have been a tacit understanding between them.

Holo pursed her lips in an arrogant manner, then broke out into a grin, one of her fangs poking out from her lips as she said, "Coral. The tree of the sea, no?"

"Yeah. What about it?"

"And what is it that the villagers hunt now?"

"That would be… Oh!"

Deer.

They were inhabitants of the forest, branch-like antlers growing from their heads.

"And what you said when you sold that rancid powder."

69

The sulfur powder they got from Nyohhira was something one could dissolve in hot water and experience a hot spring.

That was what Lawrence told the villagers when he sold the powder to the townsfolk as they were elated by the upcoming festival.

They could dig a hole in the ground and make their own hot spring.

"The villagers have only survived thus far because of the tree. It matters not whose insight dictated they settle on deer hunting, because it was none other than the tree who filled their stomachs before."

"Which means we could plant some of the deer antlers in the pond, right?"

The pond he had built had, at one point, most certainly been filled with gems. With things that could actually be touched and obtained, unlike the coral, which eventually became unobtainable in the man's hometown.

"And this would be the end, yes?" Holo asked, pointing to the scripture.

Described within was a well-known scene of God bestowing faith into priests of the future.

"There's no point if Rahden doesn't become a bishop. But I think this could work."

Though Rahden and the rest of the villagers were not quite seeing eye to eye at the moment, that was not what either truly wanted. They should be walking shoulder to shoulder together into a brilliant future.

They should be able to spend many joyous days into the future, just as Lawrence and Holo found Nyohhira together.

"The villagers can show their appreciation for everything Rahden's done, and it should get across to him that they hope he takes on a new role."

"And, most importantly," Holo grinned, no trace of tears in her eyes, "it will not be long before we can have delicious trout again."

Lawrence laughed at her appetite. "That's also true," he replied.

Though Lawrence and Holo had come to their own conclusion, it was nothing more than a guess.

If things went forward without them confirming how Rahden actually felt, then things would warp even further.

The first thing the following morning, they went to the church and spoke with Elsa. Since things were getting nowhere in the present situation, Elsa agreed to go along with their plan.

And so, they decided to see how Rahden truly felt, but Holo stopped Lawrence right outside the man's room.

"I believe I should go in alone."

"What?"

"This is a delicate matter for a boy. A sweet lady such as myself will make it much easier for him to open up," she said, almost astonished that she had to explain this to him.

Yet Lawrence remained unconvinced; Elsa reached out from behind him to pat him on the shoulder.

"Leave this to her," she said.

"..."

If Elsa said so, then he had no choice but to obey.

Holo did not seem very happy about that, but she still huffed to collect herself, then went into Rahden's room.

"I hope she'll be okay… I hope she doesn't make him angry," Lawrence expressed his unease, and Elsa drew up her shoulders.

"Miss Holo is quite adept when it comes to matters such as these," she said. "But I don't understand why she acts so debauched all the time."

71

They did not have to wait very long.

Holo emerged not long after, a smug grin on her face.

"Next, the mayor."

Though it likely went well, Lawrence wondered how Rahden was doing.

He tried to peek inside, but Holo reached up and pinched his cheek.

"Look at how inconsiderate you are."

She was telling him to leave the man be. Lawrence rubbed his cheek as he reminded himself that Holo was, indeed, the wisewolf—her recent degeneracy almost made him forget.

When they proposed their idea to Sulto, Lawrence, Elsa, and the Salonia bishop were present.

When Sulto heard the idea, his eyes widened in surprise, and he forgot to breathe; he almost went completely white.

The first reason being in response to his own ignorance for not realizing that Rahden had been getting weaker.

The second reason being that he had not even considered that his urging Rahden to take a break would be seen as him trying to oust him in the eyes of the other.

It was not because Sulto was particularly dense, but simply because he respected Rahden with his entire body and soul. The other villagers were similar; they were devastated that their feelings of gratitude had been taken the wrong way this entire time.

When Lawrence explained to them what sort of event they could hold to show their gratitude to Rahden, they all looked like desert-dwellers who had seen the rain for the first time in ten years.

Having finally learned how Rahden felt, the matter of becoming a bishop fell by the wayside, and they prioritized showing the man just how grateful they were for him.

The idea of doing this in the village pond came up, but considering how people would come and go from it, they decided putting deer antlers inside it was not very good for the possibility of the hatchery's revival, and Holo insisted that it be done in a livelier, more exciting manner, so they decided to hold it in Salonia.

Just like Laud, there were many in town who remembered the hunger that was kept at bay thanks to Rahden. When Lawrence brought up the idea to Laud, the merchant readily volunteered to find laborers to dig holes.

Lawrence then snuck in his merchant's craftiness and his opinions as a bathhouse owner.

"You want us to make an impromptu pond into a hot spring?"

Laud, of course, immediately recognized that Lawrence was trying to sell them sulfur, and he made sure to convey that in his gaze.

"Rahden's knees are going bad, you see. Why do you think hot-spring cures are so popular with the elderly?"

When Lawrence asked, Laud blinked.

"Because it helps, right? I know the rumors—it's like a panacea."

"In reality, that's a bit of an exaggeration, but I do believe you will see solid results."

Merchants were a curious lot. Laud leaned forward, interested.

"A body floats in the water, doesn't it?" Lawrence went on. "In hot springs, you can even move around like you're still young."

Laud nodded, interested.

"And," Lawrence continued, "I do want Lord Rahden to experience this, but—"

Laud cleared his throat. "If we are to dig a hole, make it into a hot spring, and hold this event during the festival, then we'll need to establish groundwork in all relevant fields. Since you

73

recommend I purchase a lot of your sulfur, then how do you feel about this for commission?"

He produced an abacus from his belt and quickly set the beads into a particular place.

With a smile, Lawrence reached over and moved some around.

"Hmm... Very well, then. I suppose I'll order some drinks that will go with our impromptu baths."

Lawrence and Laud shook on it. When Lawrence turned to look at Holo, who had been watching the exchange, she only gave him an exasperated shrug.

Baum hopped onto his horse to return to the village and fetch deer antlers that looked like coral. While he was there, he would also tell the rest of the villagers to come to town.

And since Lawrence was a bathhouse owner, he busied himself with work, directing workers as they lay bricks in the hole they had dug by the river. Holo sat not too far away on a blanket, sipping her drinks as she watched and occasionally writing things down in her diary.

Rahden showed up on the second day, and there was a scene as the villagers tried to stop him from helping. He must have been the sort to always keep himself busy in one way or another for peace of mind. Lawrence gave him the job of hammering down the bottom of the holes to firm up the ground. That way, his knees were protected, and Rahden indeed did a wonderful job.

The final day of the market came at last, and people began turning their attention to the festival.

Salonia's bishop took charge of the affair, and thus began a little festival to celebrate all those who worked hard to bring food besides the loathsome herring to the tables of all those not just in Salonia, but in the surrounding communities as well.

They poured boiled river water into the holes, and they filled them with Lawrence's sulfur.

First, the village children performed a little play that told Rahden's story, of his voyage from Rahdelli to where the village was now, in front of the pond. Baum was in charge up until the point Rahden came to Salonia.

The story then shifted to the present Rahden.

Rahden's face was bright red as he sat silently—he was likely embarrassed—and Sulto came to kneel before him.

"Lord Rahden, this is for you."

What he handed to him was a hook seemingly combined with the crest of the Church.

"Please draw up a gem from this lake with your faith."

Rahden looked as though he was about to start yelling at any moment, but he looked like this because he was tensing his face in order to keep from crying. He took the hook made from the Church crest in hand and stood up.

His movements were powerful; it was hard to imagine that his knees were not in the best shape.

But before he took a step, he turned to Sulto and said, "My knees are no good. May I borrow your shoulder?"

Sulto nodded, eyes wide, and the villagers rushed forward, offering to be his support.

Then, with the entire village surrounding him, Rahden tossed the hook into the water. He had done this once upon a time, every day, from sunup to sundown at the sea in his hometown, and not once in three years had he found any coral.

But there were plenty of deer antlers submerged in the water.

This was proof of people's livelihood, the very same Rahden had come to preserve at the end of his long journey.

"Behold! A divine miracle!"

Salonia's bishop spoke in a booming voice, befitting his station, and the antlers were brought up to the side of the pond. There was a deafening cheer and applause, and the church bells rang, too. Overcome with emotion, Rahden turned to Sulto to express his thanks.

But it was not quite time for that yet.

"Lord Rahden."

The one who appeared was Elsa—the spitting image of a servant of God, whose stiff expression did not falter even in the midst of a celebration.

"Here."

She politely handed him the selection of passages from the scripture, translated by Col, open to a specific page.

"This is…"

Baum appeared before the perplexed tree of a man.

There was something odd resting on his shoulders.

"Lord Rahden! Take this, too!"

He practically shoved into Rahden's arms a net. It was a fishing net, one he had used at the hatchery.

With the scripture booklet in one hand, and the fishing net in the other, Rahden looked confused.

Then, Salonia's bishop appeared with feigned ignorance and said, "Rahden, devout follower of God. He speaks to you in accordance to scripture."

Rahden inhaled, waiting for the next passage.

"Set aside your fishing net, which you use to take in fish. Now you must become a fisherman who will take in people… How does that sound?"

That phrase was what God said to a legendary saint who spread God's teachings.

The phrasing had been more of an order in the scripture, but the bishop was not ordering Rahden around, and it suited how the bishop spoke.

When the bishop said that, Rahden smiled with a cough, hunched over, and pressed the scripture and fishing net to his chest.

"I will do…as you command."

Sulto and the other villagers, who had been watching with bated breath, erupted into a cheer.

They all lifted the massive man into the air.

Elsa, who knew what was happening, took the scripture booklet from him.

Rahden covered his eyes as he smiled, and the villagers tossed him into the air.

"Now, into the famous waters of the hot spring village, Nyohhira!"

Rahden was tossed into the water with a big splash. Now no one could tell if another was crying.

The entertainers then began to play their instruments, and food and drink were brought out.

Lawrence felt his eyes watering, a reaction ill-suited to his age, as he watched the villagers laugh with delight—some indulging in a full-body soak while others tentatively dipped their toes in— when someone tapped him on the arm.

"Dear, there is not enough food or drink."

Holo, who already had lamb skewers in her mouth, extended her right hand to him.

Lawrence's shoulders dropped and took her hand.

She stood prim and proper like a princess, and he stood beside her, gripping her hand tightly.

This was her place—a most precious spot for her to rest amid the torrent of time.

And from her favorite spot, she looked up to Lawrence and said, "Why don't you become a fisherman so that you may net plenty of coins? For me?"

Lawrence opened his mouth to speak, but he decided not to. He smiled, and with a sigh he replied, "Of course. As you wish."

Holo grinned, baring her canines.

The festival mood had come early to Salonia.

Perhaps it was written in the annals that within the crowd was a former traveling merchant who was simply no match for his young wife.

SUMMER'S HARVEST AND WOLF

This is a tale of when Col and Myuri still lived in the bathhouse.

◇◇

Though winter stays were most popular in the hot spring village of Nyohhira, summer saw its fair share of business as well.

Its mountainous location made it cool all year round. Having an ale or wine chilled in the cold rooms filled with snow that had accumulated over the winter, after taking a dip in the hot baths, was a temptation difficult to resist for the sinful alcoholics. That said, there were fewer people visiting in summer than in the winter, and the musicians and dancers had their own businesses to attend to in their homelands, so they were not present. This made summer a rather mild, but relatively lively season to visit Nyohhira.

The guests staying at the Spice and Wolf bathhouse, too, had all gone fishing together, so that made for a quiet morning at the establishment.

"*Haaa...*"

Holo gave a big yawn; after seeing the guests off, she lay her favorite blanket down in front of the hearth, draped a thin throw over her shoulders, and curled up like a sleepy hound. Her wolf tail, which was typically constricted and hidden when others were around, thumped against the floor in great delight, and she snored quietly. A soft heat wafted from the gently smoldering embers, a perfect complement to Nyohhira's cool summers. And of course, sitting beside Holo was a cup of some alcoholic beverage for her to sip when she awoke.

Holo was so devoted to her daily routine of debauchery, and that made bathhouse owner Lawrence smile slightly. He gazed out the open window, thinking that perhaps tomorrow would be a better day for all the little tasks he had to take care of. He should take a page out of Holo's book and learn to enjoy these peaceful moments.

With that thought in mind, he came to sit beside Holo, running his hand through her beautiful flaxen hair and stroking her wolf ears. Her eyes popped open in slight irritation, but she soon shifted to place her head on his lap.

And her tail began to sway happily once again.

If only moments like these would last forever.

Right after that thought crossed Lawrence's mind, the inn door was flung open with a slam, accompanied by a girl's loud and energetic voice.

"Big news! Listen! You have to hear what I just learned!"

Loud footsteps then began to shake the floor, and the girl's voice grew frantic.

"Brother! Where are you?! Broootheeer!"

The voice belonged to their daughter, Myuri. It was not long ago that they celebrated her coming of age with all their close friends, yet she was as rambunctious as always.

"What is that little fool on about now...?"

Though she and her daughter were near-mirror images of each other, the centuries-old Holo did not sound too pleased about the ordeal.

"Well, she sounds eager to tell us something. You don't think she's plotting some prank again, is she?"

"She called for little Col, though."

The boy Col, who Lawrence and Holo met while they were traveling together, was now a valuable individual who supported the bathhouse's operations, and one whom Myuri looked up to as her older brother. They were family.

"I guess it'd be weird for her to ask for Col if she were plotting a prank."

But the way she was stomping about gave Lawrence a bad feeling and he furrowed his brow; Holo, still laying down, reached for her glass of booze that sat next to her.

Her ears then stood on end all of a sudden, and she gave a disgruntled sigh. The reasons for which did not take long to manifest.

"Mother! Father! Where are you?!"

It was unusual for Myuri to call for her parents, considering how much they scolded her, which earned a heavy sigh from Holo. This could not be a good thing.

Just before lunch, Lawrence armed himself with a bag filled with sausage, a pot, and a large hemp sack strapped to his person. Standing beside him was Col, who carried a sack full of bread and, strangely enough, a copy of the scripture under his arm.

"Safe travels. Bring back something special to share."

Hanna, the woman in charge of the kitchen, saw Lawrence and Col off with the same enthusiasm as she did the guests who went fishing earlier this morning.

The one who gave the most enthusiastic response and a wave of the hand was Myuri as she dashed ahead. Holo followed behind, a vexed look on her face, though she did seem to be enjoying herself, all things considered. The boys, carrying all the luggage, were behind them.

"Hey, sorry, Col, for making you do this on your day off."

"Oh, no, I should be apologizing to you, Mister Lawrence."

Though they apologized to each other, the one who was truly at fault was Myuri.

"There's a demon in the mountains?"

Myuri, her eyes gleaming, her silver wolf ears and tail fidgeting in excitement, had come to her parents to ask just that. Apparently, some of the village children who had ventured into an untouched part of the mountain had come back alarmed and flush-faced.

"The mountain is Mother's territory, right? If there's a demon here, we have to get rid of it!"

She loved tales of adventure; she had taken a branch in hand and was swinging it around like a sword. Col and Lawrence exchanged glances—this was when they would typically scold her for behaving immaturely, but in a surprising twist, it was Holo who spoke up this time.

"It rained not long ago, no? There should be plenty of mushrooms sprouting in the mountains."

The one who held the most sway in the bathhouse was not its owner, but Holo, who had a very short leash on her husband.

And so, they all ended up going mushroom picking together.

"Brother! Father! Hurry up!"

Myuri dashed ahead along the almost imperceptible mountain path. The trek was not a problem for Holo, either, and she proceeded forward with light steps. They were wolf parent and child, of course, but not only were Lawrence and Col merely human, they were also saddled with baggage.

They were so breathlessly concentrated on keeping up that they soon lost their way.

"We'd have to live out the rest of our lives in the woods if we make either of them angry..."

"Ha-ha-ha..." Col laughed dryly.

"But," Lawrence continued, "what did she mean by *demon*?"

Myuri had apparently called for Col first right after rushing home for good reason. Col had once studied, and still studied, theology; he wanted to be a priest in the future.

It seemed she'd thought he would be perfect for exorcising demons.

"I'm not sure... Anyone could mistake a deer or a rabbit for one if they ventured into the mountains in the middle of the night in a test of courage."

"Hmm... Oh, there's a marker. The village kids must have left this here."

The paths the adults used to take into the mountains were relatively safe, but the adventurous spirit of the unruly children lay beyond unmarked paths.

"We don't even come around here during hunting season," Col remarked.

"I hope it's not too far from here..."

Lawrence readjusted the packs on his back, following after the carefree wolf tails as they slipped through the trees.

After trekking for a little longer, the contrasting furs finally stopped moving.

"Phew... Is this it?"

"Yeah, I think so."

Even though Myuri wasn't carrying anything, she had not broken a sweat at all.

As Lawrence pulled out a waterskin full of booze—for Holo, who he knew was going to start begging him for a drink any moment now—he asked, "What did you mean by demon? A bear, or something?"

"What...? By demon, I mean demon! No one would confuse a demon with a bear, obviously."

Indeed, the village children would not get their animals wrong. In that case, it might be a recluse who dressed as a demon. Occasionally, in remote mountains such as this, there lived people who could not find a place living alongside others.

"Is there anyone around?" Lawrence asked Holo as she took a swig of wine from the waterskin, and her ears stood on end.

"That little fool would pick up on them if there were." After wiping a drop of wine that clung to the corner of her mouth on Lawrence's clothes, she stretched. "Mmm. What a nice spot. 'Tis not far from the bathhouse. There must be more nice spots like this."

People came to the mountain to either hunt animals or forage for food, so these types of places were rare.

"Then what did the children see?"

Holo did not respond to Lawrence's question. She shoved her wineskin back at Lawrence and moved to follow her daughter. Myuri led the way, pretending this was an adventure; Lawrence and Col did as Holo directed and were busy picking any mushrooms and blackberries she located.

The reason they brought a pot up was because the queen of the bathhouse had insisted they make mushroom stew for lunch.

Lawrence knew that if he told her the one who wanted the stew should carry the pot herself, he would have found himself abandoned in the mountains. As he finished that thought, he noticed Myuri standing still. She seemed to have come across a particularly large tree. The whole thing was covered in moss, and there was a hole near its roots roomy enough for one large bear to comfortably live in. It was a big, ancient tree.

"It's magnificent," he remarked.

Ignoring the way her daughter stared up at the large tree, Holo said, "Shall we eat here?"

The shadows of the forest trees told them that the sun was well past its zenith. They needed to get started, otherwise it would be sunset by the time they arrived home.

Lawrence and Col put down their things, when Myuri suddenly whirled around.

"What?! But we haven't found the demon yet!"

"The village children told you this, didn't they? You sure they weren't just teasing you?"

Lawrence asked, and Myuri puffed out her cheeks.

"Okay, okay," he sighed. "Once we're done eating, your old man'll help you find this demon."

"Aww..."

She wanted to resume her adventure right away, and she pouted, sulking. Even though she was just old enough for them to start thinking about marrying her off, she still acted like a child; this both relieved and vexed Lawrence at the same time.

Though he was delighted to watch his daughter grow up, he had recently been beset by fits of loneliness at the prospect of letting her go. He took her hand and said to her, "Let's eat first."

Myuri was just about to do as she was told, reluctantly, when her head whipped around in another direction.

"..."

To be more precise, her ears and nose were twitching slightly.

She was a young wolf who had found prey. The way she looked when this happened was breathtakingly awe-inspiring and beautiful.

Myuri, full of a youthful light that Holo simply did not possess, suddenly dashed off and rounded the large tree.

"Myuri!"

Panicked, Lawrence rushed after her, rounding the tree's roots, and found his daughter standing there.

And there he saw that the silver fur on her tail—a color she got from him—was standing on end in a way he had never seen before.

"N—"

"What?"

Myuri stood stock-still, and Col's footsteps followed as he rushed over to see what was happening.

In that moment, there came a piercing scream, one that made it seem as though the giant tree had burst.

"Eeeeeeee!"

Myuri screamed so loud that it seemed like all the hair on her tail might fall off, whirled around on her heel, and then ran.

Whatever she had seen was enough to give her a good scare.

But this was Lawrence's most beloved daughter. Though she'd grown standoffish after coming of age, Lawrence knew he should still comfort her in her fear; he spread his arms wide to accept her, but she ran straight past him.

"Brotheeer!"

"Wh-what's going on?!"

"Brother, Brother! It's the demon! The demon's here!"

Lawrence could hear Myuri crying in Col's arms behind him.

Col was holding her tightly, trying to soothe her out of her fear.

Though as beautiful a bond between brother and sister it was, Lawrence wasn't sure what to do with his spread arms. He supposed he wasn't the one she went to for help anymore.

As he stood there, disappointed, he heard the approaching sound of crunching leaves.

It was Holo, peering up at him with a mean smile.

"You fool."

She grinned, grabbed Lawrence's awkwardly outstretched arms, and pulled him closer.

The shrewd wisewolf walked off, pulling Lawrence by the arm as she did so. She took him to where Myuri had been standing and Lawrence found himself freezing in place.

A demon was trying to crawl out from the ground.

"Oh, whoa—"

It also gave him a good fright, and he almost landed on his behind. It looked as though the pale hand of a corpse was crawling out of the ground; its nails were long and sinister, and its eerie fingers were pointed.

"Wh-what is—?"

He did not honestly think that a demon was coming out from the mountain. As he stood with his breath held, Holo let go of him, crouched down besides the hand, and reached out to touch the demon's fingers.

And after a firm poke, its finger snapped.

"You fool. 'Tis a mushroom."

"What?!"

Disregarding Lawrence's shock, Holo burst out in laughter, her shoulders shaking as she did so.

"Heh-heh-heh… Were you petrified by a *mushroom*?" she cackled, waving her hand as she stood. "But once, long ago, I thought someone had been buried alive when I spotted one in the woods and tried to dig them out."

"Y-you did?"

"It looked just like the hand of a corpse, you know. I have a feeling 'tis called by a similar name."

One of the fingers had broken off when Holo poked it, but that did not make it seem any less like the pale hand of a demon.

"But I suppose 'tis rather rare for a corpse's hand to look this clean."

It sounded as though she was trying to cheer him up when a thought suddenly occurred to Lawrence.

"You knew it was a mushroom all along?"

"Perhaps I did, and perhaps not."

She shrugged, turning around to grab Lawrence's hand and drag him away.

"Come now, 'tis time to eat. No one has come up this way yet, so the largest mushrooms are all ours for the harvesting. We must also gather some for Hanna once we are finished eating. I am quite looking forward to having some pickled, salted, and dried."

Lawrence found himself both exasperated and smiling in response to Holo's upbeat musings.

Or perhaps he was pleasantly surprised to know that there were all sorts of mysteries left in the world; he had not come to know everything about the world, after all.

"But…"

Lawrence contemplated. When he saw Col sitting next to the pot, deftly preparing their food with Myuri on his lap, he groaned. He wondered if Myuri was a bit too attached to her brother.

As he stood there, an uneasy impatience nagging at him, Holo tugged on his sleeve.

"Is something the matter?"

If he openly expressed his jealousy over Myuri, Holo would surely taunt him for being a fool again.

He had dignity to maintain, both as a father and a husband.

"Nothing, actually."

"Mm."

She smiled at him, her all-knowing wisewolf smile, but she did not poke him any further.

They then lit the fire, boiled plenty of mushrooms in their pot, then found plenty more to take home.

It was summer in Nyohhira.

It was a good season, where the cool breeze offered relief from the strong rays of the sun.

AN
OLD HOUND'S
SIGH AND
WOLF

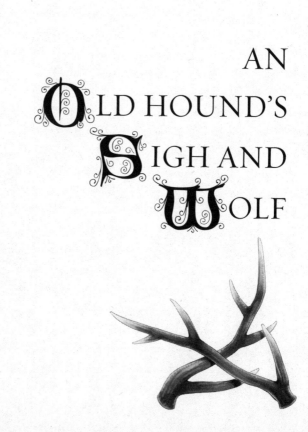

One day, a saint sent by God built a hermitage on a stretch of land that was once home to a scattered farming village. Starved of God's love, many came to visit the hermitage, which became a place for locals to trade, which in turn attracted merchants. Before any realized it, a village had sprung up around the hermitage, and in time, it grew into a town.

This was the basic premise of Salonia's creation myth, but a traveling merchant acquaintance told her that the likeliest story was that a charismatic individual who was not quite who they claimed to be came to live in the area, jumped on the bandwagon to develop the area, and made it look like a town, at least superficially. When priestess Elsa first heard that, she thought, *How typical*, as she scanned Salonia's busy streets with honey-colored eyes.

Elsa originally lived in a village very far from Salonia, but she left her family behind to visit various churches around the world. These churches were no longer keeping up with the ways of the world and were struggling to adapt to the times, which made people with sharp executive abilities like her a necessity. She had eventually found herself here, happily moving from place to place as the Church demanded; she was, of course, a very pious woman.

But hearing the truth behind Salonia's creation myth was chilling because it served as a reminder that there were very few things in this world that were genuine.

And so, she was not surprised when she saw that Salonia's church had been left in the care of a bishop who was vaguely untrustworthy. And when money trouble once again reared its ugly head, all she could do was give a little sigh.

"Someone seems irritated, no?"

Salonia was currently gripped by excitement for the festival that would be the high point of their grand market, yet Elsa sat under the eaves of an out-of-the-way tavern nestled in a quiet side street; she looked up when she heard the familiar voice speak to her.

"Fancy seeing you here."

The young girl with flaxen hair did not bother to reply to Elsa's statement, nor did she bother to ask permission to sit with Elsa before taking a seat opposite her and calling over the tavern-keeper in a practiced manner.

The mismatch of her sage-like demeanor and her youthful appearance stemmed from the fact that she was currently inhabiting a temporary form. She was, in fact, a centuries-old wolf spirit, and whenever Elsa looked at her, it always struck her how much the way she thought about wolves had changed ever since they met.

She didn't know if this was a good or bad thing, but she was certain that this wolf avatar would be furious with her if she shared these thoughts with her.

"'Tis quite a shock to find you in such a desolate, sad place," Holo said, accepting the wine and the meat-and-vegetable stew the tavernkeeper brought her.

"Because this stew is delicious. And it is quiet here."

"Ah, yes. You are no pompous official of the Church. You are a village girl."

Elsa felt rather embarrassed still being called a "girl" after having three children of her own, but perhaps their meeting decades ago felt like a recent development to a spirit who had lived for centuries.

She brought her ale up to her lips as the thought crossed her mind.

"And you are well off enough to be drinking at lunch."

"Even God set aside one day for rest. I am simply doing what I am meant to be doing." Holo frowned—Elsa typically scolded her for her heavy drinking and slovenly lifestyle—then bit into the overcooked chicken, cartilage and all, baring her canines. "I am just as surprised as you are. Where is Mister Lawrence?"

This wolf spirit, who once ruled over a village's wheat harvest, through some sort of divine grace came to marry an airy merchant. Having had a small hand in bringing them together, Elsa was happy to see that they always got along so well, but they were unfortunately so close that it was almost unpleasant sometimes.

Or perhaps they were so close that they ended up fighting again—and just as that possibility occurred to Elsa, Holo let her shoulders fall the way a much older woman might have, and responded as she sipped her wine.

"He's quite popular here. He's always gone somewhere once the sun rises."

Her wolf ears, hidden beneath her headkerchief, twitched in displeasure.

This wolf was surprisingly shy and a loner to boot; she must have decided she would much rather sit with someone she found annoying because of all the lectures instead of wandering the town alone.

"He has indeed solved a few big problems thus far, hasn't he?"

First there was the enormous, complicated matter of debt that had weighed upon the people of Salonia. Merchants who had come to the market for trade had been unable to repay their borrowed money, yet he had been able to erase almost all of that debt without spending a single coin—it was hardly distinguishable from magic at that point.

That was more than enough to go down in the town's history, yet he had even resolved a problem involving the man who had established a fish pond that had once saved Salonia from starvation. It was under Lawrence's direction that they dug a hole in the town plaza to make a little pond reminiscent of the sea that served as the stage for a little play.

They poured hot water into the freshly dug pond and filled it with a hot spring mix brought from Nyohhira, turning it into a place where the adults could soak their feet and the children could play to their hearts' content; it added a touch of color to the market's excitement.

Of course, Holo had always stood by Lawrence's side as he solved these problems. The people knew her as the great merchant Kraft Lawrence's young wife, who kept her husband on a short leash, projected a powerful presence, and could hold her liquor like no other; Elsa was certain that Holo was plenty popular in her own right.

"I would think *you* have had plenty of invitations to go drinking yourself, no?"

It was not long ago that Holo had been tasked with choosing the drinks that would be served at the festival that marked the end of the seasonal festival, which ended with her dead-drunk in the middle of the day.

She would certainly have no trouble finding others to drink with now. And considering how her love of alcohol was second to none, Elsa thought she would have little reason to decline an invitation, yet the woman sitting across from her turned away, an unmistakable weariness in her expression.

"'Twas only fun in the beginning."

"Too much attention, I take it?"

As self-important as she seemed, Holo preferred to be alone. Yet she hated being put on a pedestal. The pagan gods were all similarly difficult to understand, but perhaps that was what made them who they were.

Elsa brought her cup of lukewarm ale to her lips to find it was mostly empty.

She had finished her lunch; perhaps it was time to return to the church.

As that thought crossed her mind, she noticed how Holo was glumly sipping at her wine, having only bitten into her chicken and made no progress on her stew at all.

When she saw how anxiously the wolf sat hunched over on her spot, Elsa knew she could not leave her be.

She sighed. She was astonished at how little had changed with this wisewolf since they first met, yet that also brought her considerable relief.

"More wine, please!" Elsa ordered, raising up her empty mug toward the inside of the building, and Holo's eyes widened when she did so.

"I know if you simply had nothing to do, you would be back at your room at the inn sleeping. You want to speak with me, don't you?"

Holo was centuries old and was even known as the wisewolf, yet here she was—shoulders drawn up and tensed, lips pursed. Elsa thought about how much this wolf looked like her own children.

Holo peered up at Elsa, as though she had been waiting for her to say something like that.

"…Will you not laugh at me?"

Though the role was temporary, Elsa was still a priestess.

"I cannot call myself a servant of God if I laugh at the plight of others."

Holo still looked away briefly, downed the rest of her wine in a single gulp, and ordered herself another, not wanting to fall behind.

Many villagers would have knelt before her in ages past, honored with words of prophecy or whatever else they would like to hear; but now, as she sat hunched over her cup of wine, Holo looked like a village elder who had grown so old she seemed like a child again.

"That fool does not understand a single thing about me."

Elsa absently thought about how this was essentially her catch-phrase, yet she urged Holo to continue out of slight interest.

"What do you mean?"

"Do you know that he has been summoned to take part in some complicated discussions?"

"Oh?"

Lawrence was presently the most famous individual in Salonia, and many likely thought that any problem in his care would be solved immediately. She had heard that he was being made to intervene in anything and everything from business dealings to marital disputes; she wondered which one it could be this time.

"I have heard it is related to your job."

"Ah-ha." Elsa understood immediately. "Is this about the town tariffs?"

"I am not quite sure. But I hear tell of merchants just like him butting heads with one another."

"I've heard the same."

Holo's brow furrowed, perhaps dissatisfied with Elsa's casual response.

But Elsa, too, gave a sigh, and Holo stared blankly at her.

"That very same problem is why I am not looking forward to returning to the church. It's quite a stupid situation."

That was why she had gone out of her way to have lunch here; without warning, Elsa heard the rhythmic rustling of fur against fabric.

"Oh ho?"

Holo had seemed so lifeless not moments earlier, but her energy came back the moment she saw how troubled Elsa looked. Her fluffy tail was wagging with delight beneath her clothes. Elsa could hardly believe the woman, but she did not hate how open and frank she was.

"Discussions about the tariffs for all the goods that flow into town are going on at the assembly hall right now. I suppose it would be easier for you to understand if I told you this meeting would determine whether that wine of yours would be a cheap or expensive drink."

Holo looked down at the mug in her hands, then gulped down the wine along with the information.

"There are wine merchants who wish to import the wine for cheap, and there are the ale merchants who wish to subject wine to higher tariffs since that is their competition."

"Mm."

"Though who exactly manages these clashes of interest changes from town to town. Here, it is the church's responsibility."

Elsa supposed that part of the reason for this was because a saint had a hand in the town's founding myth, but in truth, the church was heavily involved in the process because they earned great profits from those tariffs.

"Ah, yes, the one in charge of the church here is a fishy sort. He is quite fun to drink with, but I suppose you're not too fond of him."

"He's not a bad person, but unfortunately, he's always been a bit of a smooth talker…"

The entity that originally called on Elsa to help was the church in the Vallan Bishopric. There she had reunited with Lawrence and Holo, gotten their help, and managed to sell off a lot of the church's assets for a high price. The bishop in Salonia had caught wind of this and managed to shove all of Salonia's problems onto Elsa. The work itself was not a problem for her, but she was not exactly happy with the situation. This feeling was exacerbated by the enormous profits the Salonia church claimed for itself despite ostensibly being an establishment meant to preach and practice asceticism and temperance.

Elsa realized she had unwittingly spoken ill of him when she did not mean to; she cleared her throat and found Holo grinning at her, canines and all.

"*Ahem.* Anyway, all interests regarding money will be laid bare at this meeting, and everyone will be desperate to speak their piece. And I believe that Mister Lawrence has been saddled with that responsibility, and his opinion carries great weight…"

Perhaps the reason Holo looked so upset was because she was sad that he was not around to entertain her. Elsa thought that if that were truly the case, then she would simply say so, but she knew well that the pair tended not to be very honest with their feelings with each other and needlessly suffered because of it at times.

They were two peas in a pod, yes, but she thought it would do them good if they could at least put themselves in each other's shoes.

"I understand he has an important role to play in this town, yes. And he has done more than enough to atone for the sin of leaving me by my lonesome," Holo said proudly, and Elsa decided to give nothing more than a vague hum in response. The wise-wolf continued, saying, "But the problem is that he dives head-first into these problems in the first place."

"Is that so? It is true that this is causing the townsfolk great distress, and it must be resolved at some point. As an outsider, Mister Lawrence is perfectly suited to settle the town's disagreements. I believe he is fulfilling his role rather well, and you must be proud of his accomplishments, are you not?"

"Yes, 'tis true…," Holo muttered.

Elsa sighed and said, "I believe Mister Lawrence is doing all this to show you just how capable he actually is."

Ever since reuniting at the church in the Vallan Bishopric, just from looking Elsa could tell that Holo was practically all that Lawrence ever thought about, and she could easily see from everything he did that he was in high spirits about his first journey in ten years.

And though she thought that this selfish maiden quite liked that part about him, the wolf herself gave a heavy sigh.

"…This is the third time in a row now. I feel a burp coming on."

Holo reminded Elsa of an old neighborhood stray who grew languid after receiving too much attention from the children.

Elsa could tell that Holo was disappointed, but she felt as though the answer to this problem was plain as day.

"Why not tell him this? You are not a newlywed wife," she told her outright, and Holo simply hunched over and sipped her wine.

"'Twould be easy if I could do such a thing. In a way…I am the one who encouraged the fool in the first place…"

Though in her true form she was a wolf big enough to decimate entire armies, she would tuck her tail between her legs in fear of a single ex-merchant, and Elsa found that very curious.

As that thought crossed Elsa's mind, interest bubbled up inside her—what sort of trap had this wolf gotten herself ensnared in this time?

"How so?"

Though she sat up straighter, Holo tensed her shoulders and neck, gazing into empty space, and spoke again with the umpteenth sigh, "You had a hand in bringing him and I together."

Elsa's eyes widened despite herself; she was not so much confused about why Holo suddenly brought this up, but more in shock from Holo suddenly thanking her.

"Do not make that face... 'Twas by your encouragement that we joined hands. You know this."

When Elsa rode in the same carriage as Holo, the main reason Holo had seemed so uncomfortable was because she was aware of just how much of a debt she owed the church woman.

"Either way, we are together now. In truth, I am happy. Painfully so."

"I...suppose you are, yes. And to be honest, Mister Lawrence spoils you too much."

The centuries-old wolf replied, with good grace, "He does so because he wants to."

"Even so..."

Though it had only been a bit more than a decade since they started a family together, they were naturally much closer now than they were when they first met.

Elsa took a sip of her own wine, washing down the sweet sentimentality.

"But one could say that me taking his hand was the same as pulling him away from the path he wished to pursue, no?"

"Hmm... Perhaps."

If anything, Elsa thought it would be more apt to say that it was not a wise idea to leave Lawrence to his own devices, considering how shaky the man could be sometimes, but it sounded as though Holo had her own thoughts on the matter.

"Are you saying that you made a mistake?"

"…He had the chance to follow a path that would have led him to becoming the world's greatest merchant, one who could rule the world. But I said to him that I'd had enough of such nonsense and steered him away from it."

That was not a sphere of livelihood that overlapped much with Elsa's own, so she was only vaguely aware of such things, but she knew that Lawrence had saved one of the biggest, most influential companies in the northlands and had been invited to join them.

Had he accepted, it was very likely his wit and Holo's wisdom together could have made him an unimaginably wealthy man in some city or another.

That said, Elsa had a hard time picturing Lawrence as a big name, lording over dozens and dozens of people. She thought that the size of the bathhouse in Nyohhira was perfect for him, but perhaps that was not the case for Holo.

As Elsa dropped her shoulders—*Love is truly blind*, she thought—Holo spoke up.

"And…I found myself expressing this to him."

"…"

Elsa's own thoughts about how foolish that was must have been plain on her face. With a pained expression, Holo growled, baring her fangs.

Elsa sighed and cleared her throat at the same time, then looked straight at Holo and said, "Mister Lawrence prefers his life with you over everything else, and so he has internalized your wishes. I doubt he regrets his choice."

"I know!"

Nearby birds flew away, shocked by Holo's sharp yell.

She repeated, annoyed, "I know," and dropped her head into her hands. "I had been too relaxed once we left for our first journey in years... And I had so much time to think in the cart, at nights in the inns... And most importantly..." She stared down at the table. "When I see him lit by the glow of unfamiliar hearths, I see just how much he has aged in the time we have spent together. I never notice that in the familiar confines of the bathhouse."

Holo still looked like a young girl, much the same as she did when Elsa first met her, and she would likely remain the same when Elsa was old enough to need a cane. In her eyes, ten, twenty years was nothing more than a short temporal detour.

But that was not the case for Lawrence.

As they traveled around in the same fashion as they had when they first met, Holo couldn't help but notice the undeniable signs of age in his impulses, in the fires that illuminated his profile.

Elsa knew that Holo walked around with pen and paper, writing down things that happened in her daily life.

It was an act meant to commit certain moments to memory that would be otherwise washed away by the unrelenting torrent of time.

Elsa could no longer laugh or find exasperation when it came to Holo; she reached out across the table and placed her hand over the wolf's own small hand.

"I realize that he has given me something so great." Holo stared at the hand on hers before pulling it away with a self-deprecating smile. "We visited your company, the Debau Company? When we sold your mountain. How dizzyingly large it was. It was a bustling, dazzling place, so full of life. When I think about how I stole him away from such a life...I am overcome with fear."

Elsa, too, was from a small village called Tereo, so she could

easily imagine the sort of shock that Holo experienced. She had been shocked by her own drive to make a name for herself in the world, one she had never felt before she first laid eyes on a massive cathedral in a large city.

Of course, that was now but a vestige of a dream that perhaps could have come true once; she knew that much of the appeal would be lost if she were to actually achieve it, and there was no guarantee that she would have the same wonderful things in life if she had decided to walk a different path.

The journey of life was a cruel one with no do-overs. Everyone was forced to keep walking forward while forever wondering if the choices they made were the right ones.

Holo would live for a very, very long time, so perhaps at some point she would have accepted these facts with little more than a sense of defeat, but when it came to her most beloved companion, she simply could not keep a level head.

That said, Elsa doubted Lawrence ever regretted for a moment the choices that led him to his current life, and she knew that saying anything she was not wholly confident in would be a disservice to him. He was so loved, and so she felt it was his responsibility to believe wholly and with conviction that his partner was happy, too.

As a member of the clergy, Elsa would often serve as mediator for when married couples had disputes. She had seen similar situations play out thousands of times before. A lecture almost bubbled out from her throat—*You will live tens of times longer than any human, so why do you find yourself caught up by the most basic of entrapments?*—but Holo seemed perfectly aware of her own foolishness.

Not only that, but there were particulars that only applied to her.

Elsa, who acted as intermediary for this odd couple, forcefully dragged Holo's hand back to hers and gave it an encouraging squeeze before letting it go.

"I see what's going on."

The town believed Holo dragged Lawrence around on a short leash, and at a glance it did seem as though Lawrence was completely at the mercy of Holo's whims, but it was actually Holo who could scarcely bear to be away from Lawrence.

Then again, Lawrence was not the fairy-tale prince he seemed to be at all.

"I suppose it's like thoughtlessly adding sugar to mead, which is already perfectly sweet enough."

When Elsa said that, Holo looked genuinely disappointed.

"Precisely. And now, he is approaching me with a large jar of sugar and a big grin on his face. And I thought my slip of the tongue had died with the complicated issue of debts. I so foolishly told him that he could have easily become a great merchant with his magic, considering how easily he had made all that debt disappear."

Childish though she was, it was more than enough to dispel Holo's fears, and her joy certainly would have been great.

There was a caveat to this, though, Elsa thought. She did not immediately associate Lawrence with being a sheep because of his softheartedness, but because he did not know his limits; because he was at times inconsiderate and thickheaded.

"After seeing how well it went, he now wants to settle this tariff matter cleanly and show you how capable he is, is that correct?" Elsa asked.

Holo gave a long, deep sigh.

"...Yes."

Elsa could see how a man might want to continually show off for his beloved wife.

As a servant of God, she thought it was a good thing that they were so close, that it was a good wife's job to be impressed by and compliment her husband, but that was simply a matter of logic.

She, too, had built a family after finding herself with a man who had a bottomless well of kindness, but was also a bit thickheaded as well.

She thought back on her days in Tereo, and easily pictured her husband, Evan, doing the same thing to her over and over again. She might certainly be delighted the first time, and perhaps she might force a smile the second time, but her patience would likely run out by the third.

"'Twould be nice if that were all, however."

"There's something else?"

"That church of yours came up. He has apparently been lured into some scheme by them."

When Holo put it that way, Elsa knew right away who was doing the smooth talking.

"The bishop, you mean?"

"Aye. That bishop has promised him a dubious reward in exchange for his help. And..." Holo brought her wine to her lips, gave an indulgent sip, and looked at Elsa with a dubious expression. "That fool has told me it would not be a bad idea to be nobility."

Men would always be children. Elsa pictured Lawrence innocently dreaming and smiling, and it reminded her of Evan when she scolded him for making a ruckus with the children.

"That fool has started to dream big again now that Myuri has left. I almost feel as though he is using my circumstances as a tool for his own advantage."

"Ah..."

Elsa sometimes heard similar complaints back in the village. The village women would often sigh, thinking they were done raising their kids, only for the largest person in the house to begin to act like a child himself.

No matter how old they got, men still acted with wide-eyed optimism, just like children. Even if that was what brought the couple together in the first place, she understood why the women would be frustrated and want them to act their age.

"And is it not strange for a sheep to walk straight for a cliff edge with a smug look on its face?"

It was not as though Holo could have opened up about any of this to her town drinking buddies, and she clearly did not have any ill will toward Lawrence himself, so she had been bottling up everything.

After a great deal of thought, she must have decided to find this alleyway tavern and pay Elsa a visit under the guise of coincidentally running into each other.

Though their personalities and lifestyles were completely different, this was why Elsa could not bring herself to hate Holo, and since they both had similar husbands and households, she could not abandon the wisewolf.

It seemed that frivolous bishop had been getting involved, too, so she could not overlook this matter as a fellow member of the clergy either. It would be unacceptable to allow the Church's reputation to fall any more than it already had.

"More drinks, please!" Elsa called as she ordered two more cups of wine.

What Holo told Elsa was not quite to the point, but she got the general gist when she applied her own knowledge to the situation.

First, many merchants were in town for the grand market at the moment, which made for a perfect opportunity to talk about plenty of longstanding issues, when the question of tariffs came up.

Wine merchants and ale merchants have always been at odds with one another, and in turn, ale merchants have always been competitors with the bakeries since they vie for the same resource. And the bakeries have traditionally never gotten along with the butchers—listening to one party's objection meant earning another party's ire.

In general, "the enemy of my enemy is my friend" was logic that was easily upheld here, so parties whose interests did not conflict often teamed up to make sure their grievances were heard, but the local lord, dressed in red, would often unilaterally make decisions when it came to these matters, so they would either leave things up to divine providence and draw straws, or allow influential members of each party to cast anonymous votes.

The Salonia church bishop often took charge here, but the church itself had its own interests in many affairs concerning the town, so the participants would not so readily listen to what they had to say, especially if they were the ones getting the short end of the stick in the resulting deal. And then, out of the blue, Lawrence appears in town, a person who has great influence but little to do with any parties involved, so everyone began to promise him rewards in an attempt to flatter and gain his favor.

The woodworkers, especially, who had been suffocated by high tariffs, had been particularly aggressive in persuading Lawrence to secure them some tax relief, but the Church profited mightily from those same tariffs, which meant that the bishop was trying to get Lawrence on his side by making absurd promises.

What he suggested was purchasing privileges for some of the land surrounding Salonia—essentially making Lawrence nobility.

"He worked quite fast."

Once Holo had informed Elsa of the general course the meeting had taken, Elsa set out to gather information on the details. Once the sun started to set, they regrouped at a tavern that bordered the town square. The town was growing even livelier as the sun threatened to vanish beneath the horizon, and so the establishment had set out several long tables and benches outside to deal with all the customers who could not fit inside. Those dressed in traveling clothes, farmers from the nearby area, and all those who had traveled in from outside joined with the townsfolk to enjoy one of the few periods of revelry throughout the year.

When these revelers spotted Elsa, they quickly fixed their posture and lowered their voices. After giving them a vague, nonchalant smile, she listened to what Holo had to report.

"Were you drinking the entire time afterward?"

By the time Elsa found Holo again, there sat on the table a cup of wine she very much doubted was Holo's first and a plate of ribs that had been licked clean.

"You fool. This is a promise to become some landowning lord, you know. I had my suspicions that the fool might be tricked again, but there is a chance he is not."

"There *is* a chance, yes."

"Rabbits do sleep in the middle of the road from time to time."

Perhaps it was because Holo had already lived for such a long time, or she was originally like this, but she tended to have a pessimistic, depressing outlook on things. Lawrence was her sun and it was his existence that brightened her days.

"And so, he has decided to look into it himself, because he cannot ignore the chance that it might be a good deal."

But Elsa wondered if the seemingly lackadaisical but surprisingly shrewd bishop would bring something like that up in such an offhand manner. It was much more likely that Lawrence was being tricked, like Holo first suspected.

Or perhaps Holo did not want to dampen Lawrence's mood when he was delighted at the prospect of being a noble, and was trying to convince herself that it was, indeed, a very good deal.

All Elsa could do was guess when it came to discord in that department, but regardless, the point of compromise she had come up with sat beside her.

"She knows a lot about this area. I went for a quick run to fetch her after we parted ways."

"Umm... I can't say I know a lot about how the human world works, though..."

The girl sitting next to Holo, shrinking into herself, was still bigger than Holo despite how much she hunched over—and her name was Tanya.

She was a squirrel avatar who had lived in the cursed mountain, the one of legend in the Vallan Bishopric that Elsa had originally needed help with. Tanya certainly seemed like she would know the area's history in the magnitude of centuries, so perhaps this was indeed the correct choice.

But in any case, Elsa thought they could have picked a better place to meet than this.

It was starting to dawn on her that the men around them were not looking at their table because a woman in holy robes—Elsa—was spending time at a place of drink and revelry. They were looking at Tanya, who had fluffy, curly hair and voluminous curves that neither Elsa nor Holo possessed.

Any man who approached with the intention of speaking to her would quickly spot Holo, who was a minor celebrity in town, and Elsa, who wore the cloth of the Church, then quickly retreat with a vague smile.

Holo did not seem to mind at all, and Tanya had not even

noticed she was being looked at to begin with, so Elsa decided not to let it bother her.

"Miss Tanya, do you know of House Voragine?"

Elsa had asked some of the Vallan Bishopric priests who were staying in town about what the bishop was planning in detail, then returned to the church to peruse the town annals. What the bishop had promised Lawrence was land and ownership privileges that once belonged to the Voragine family.

It would be a sale of the title, not a cession of it, of course, but it was still extremely difficult to buy something like privileges even with all the money in the world, so the prospect alone of being able to purchase one was almost absurd.

"Oh, yes, I do. They were quite well-known, once. It wasn't long ago, I think."

Tanya was sipping cider and nibbling on wheat bread. A dissatisfied look crossed her face; she put it down and produced a small sack filled with acorn bread she had made herself, and continued speaking, her face lighting up in delight.

"Not long ago? When exactly?"

Acorn bread was made to simply stave off hunger, so when Holo watched Tanya eat it with such delight, a sour look crossed her face as she remembered how tart and bitter it tasted.

"Umm… I think it was…before the master came. When the mountain was ruined."

"If this was before the alchemists came, then it must have been over fifty years ago, but not quite an entire century, yes?"

Non-humans like her and Holo considered such timespans to be short; Elsa mused at how Holo easily considered herself a young girl.

"I think it was a hero who took down a great serpent that slithered through the earth."

Holo's wolf ears twitched under her headkerchief.

117

That was when Elsa realized, of course, why they were looking at her like that. She was not particularly perturbed, however, and asked Tanya, "There is record of that legend in the Church annals. Did it really happen?"

"Umm… I'm not sure? I don't really like open spaces, so I rarely ever came this way. I heard about it from the people who came to dig up metal in the mountain."

"I see." Elsa nodded.

Now it was Holo's turn to speak, and she seemed somewhat jealous.

"That was not the one who protected your village?"

Tanya blinked, looking back and forth between Holo and Elsa.

Unable to respond to Holo right away, Elsa first took a sip of her wine, sour and lacking alcohol from being overheated.

"I don't know."

There was a world of meaning behind her answer.

For one thing, she was unsure if this great serpent was the same one that was worshipped as guardian spirit in her hometown of Tereo.

For another, she was unsure if the snake had indeed protected her village.

"Ah, you are a person of the Church through and through."

There were thorns in Holo's statement, and Tanya shrunk herself down, having sensed the discord in the atmosphere, but Elsa let it roll off her.

"There is no telling where it went, if it actually existed, and what it was doing in the village if it did. Personally, seeing you has partially convinced me."

"What? What did I do?"

The way grease from the grilled meat stained the corners of Holo's mouth reminded Elsa of the rest of her family and how they acted at mealtimes.

"That perhaps it decided to take a little winter's nap that turned out to be on the long side."

Before meeting Holo, Elsa had attributed a dignified quality to all the supernatural entities that made up the pagan myths across the world. But once she came across Holo and was afforded a peek into their world, she came to understand that despite a difference in senses, they were essentially the same as regular humans.

She produced a small handkerchief from her pocket, leaned across the table, wiped the corner of an annoyed Holo's mouth for her before continuing to share her thoughts. "I'm sure it would be much too lonely to sleep in a place that was too quiet."

Holo was growing more and more angry with what those words indicated, but Elsa only chuckled and turned to look at Tanya. "I suppose you wouldn't know, either, Miss Tanya. There is a myth of a great serpent in the village where I was born."

"Um... Oh!"

"But don't worry about it. I have never seen it. All that is left is a great cave where it was said to live."

Tanya still lowered her head apologetically, so Elsa continued in a matter-of-fact tone.

"Getting back on topic, due to the Voragine family's success in slaying the great serpent that once terrorized this plain, they were gifted a portion of the land and were appointed as nobility. The church here said that God loaned his power to the hero in the battle with the serpent."

Holo scoffed.

"Not once have I ever seen this God for myself."

"Indeed. I believe the myth was created so that both parties could mutually reinforce their authority. I believe the pagan threat was rather strong in the area around that time, and the Church needed a way to assert its presence here. They wanted any claim to fame, no matter how miniscule. And conversely, the

119

one labeled a hero was likely a young fighter who wanted some sort of legitimacy to rule as a lord, so it was likely he wanted the Church's backing in the matter." It was not an unusual situation, but there was one thing that stood out. "What *I* find strange is that the Voragine family held considerable interest in this town's tariffs. That, too, was because they took down the great serpent. Or so says the annals."

"Mm?" Holo furrowed her shapely brows and glanced at Tanya beside her.

It was likely that she only looked at her to see if she knew anything, but when Tanya pulled out her second piece of acorn bread, she pulled up her shoulders as though she had done something wrong.

"And it seems the Voragine family died out after one or two generations. The land, privileges, and proceeds from the tariffs were then donated to the Church. Mister Lawrence..." Elsa paused before continuing to say, "...has been promised the family's privileges, interests, the complete set of titles, and the right to live in their fortress as a reward."

"Hmm..." A hard look crossed Holo's face as she hummed in thought. "The reward is much too generous."

The look on her face told Elsa that she was convinced her kindhearted husband was about to fall for another scheme.

"This does not seem to be a simple transfer, so I cannot say much in that regard. It would cost quite a large sum. Being able to outright buy something like this would be nothing short of a miracle—not even the greatest merchant with the biggest coffers would be able to pull this off normally. So in that sense? Yes, it is very generous. If he manages to mediate this quarrel over tariffs, after all, then what the bishop is saying is that he'd be able to become a landowning noble."

"And he is quite elated." Holo gave a deep sigh, pursing her lips.

But Elsa realized that what she was seeing was not anger. Holo was not annoyed that he was being taken in by promises too good to be true. It was almost as though she was upset that she would have to dampen her companion's excitement as he found joy in a bright future.

Lawrence doted on Holo, yes, but his wife was no slouch either.

Elsa had a vague picture of what Holo was like when she ruled over the wheat harvest in her little village. It must have been an idyllic time, much like the warm scene of a child begging their mother for something before bed.

As Holo hummed in thought, Tanya, who had been munching on her acorn bread, suddenly looked up in some sort of realization. "Oh, about the serpent..."

"Did you remember something?"

"Yes, yes I did. I remember seeing people complaining that they wanted to sell all the metal they dug up, but they couldn't do very good trade with faraway lands because of the serpent. I remember that because I thought, *Serves you right.*"

There was a hint of anger in Tanya's voice, as though recalling the time when humans laid waste to the mountain. She aggressively bit into her acorn bread.

"Aye, 'twould be a problem with a big snake taking up camp in the area. I would be frightened if it were venomous."

"I have dreams about getting swallowed whole by snakes even when I see a little one."

Elsa was not entirely convinced by their conversation.

"...Do you all attack people?"

When she had been collecting stories on the pagan gods, the only time she had heard of them attacking humans was when they ravaged their sanctuaries, though there were some exceptions.

Regardless, the image of a great serpent roaming the plains randomly attacking people did not line up with the impression she had of Holo and the other non-humans she had met.

"I do no such thing." Holo gave a huffy response.

Tanya placed a finger to her chin and said, "Maybe it was stretched out over the field, sunbathing?"

When she mentioned it, both Elsa and Holo pictured the same thing.

When a snake big enough to swallow a cow whole stretched out to occupy an entire plain, its existence alone would be enough to disrupt trade in one manner or another, even if it was not doing anything particularly bad.

"When we ventured from your mountain to this city, we had quite a good view of the land, but how big would it have to be to occupy this plain?" Holo asked.

"In the stories of the pagan gods that I collected, I found a tale of snake long enough where the weather at its head was different from the weather at its tail," Elsa said.

"If such a snake did exist, then it could have constricted and killed the Moon-hunting Bear."

Holo was right, but Elsa noticed how upset Tanya seemed— she was the one who brought up the snake because she thought it might prove useful—so she quickly changed the topic.

"E-either way, an abnormally large serpent slithering about would make it just as difficult to carry out simple trade. It makes perfect sense that the Hero Voragine vanquishing the serpent made it possible for trade to resume. It also makes sense that the right to collect tariffs was also collateral in the situation."

After throwing Elsa a cautious glance, Tanya gave her a relieved smile.

"Well, I don't quite understand, but it sounds as though some benefits gained from old efforts are being dangled before that fool's eyes. Yet...lordship, was it? Could the fool even afford something so outrageous? 'Tis not as though we are selling the bathhouse in Nyohhira..."

"What?! Are you going to live here, Lady Holo?" Tanya's eyes widened in surprise, joy coloring her eyes. "I would be so happy if you lived nearby!"

"You fool, that would nev—Actually, I do not know. I do not know. Do not make that face at me."

The mountain Tanya had so peacefully lived on had been ravaged when it was developed for mining, and when the veins ran dry, she started replanting trees, little by little. It was then that she became friends with alchemists who happened to drop by, but they, too, left without any word as to where they ended up, and she had been waiting happily for their return all the while.

Naturally, she had attached herself to Holo, and Holo, too, worried about her.

Though Tanya looked older than Holo, Holo soothed her as though she were a much larger, younger sister. The sight was silly enough to earn them a smile from Elsa; as she did so, she spotted a small group of people beyond the non-human pair. They were well-dressed merchants, having just emerged from the assembly hall, which played host to a very important meeting here in Salonia. They exchanged handshakes, stretched and pounded their backs after escaping such a long meeting.

Elsa spotted a familiar figure among the crowd, and Holo sniffed before turning around.

"As much as I am loathe to admit it, I suppose we have no choice but to hear the fool's side of the story."

The sun was beginning to set, and lanterns were being lit throughout the plaza. Though the crowd made it hard to see anything well, three women sitting outside a tavern stood out like a sore thumb. Lawrence noticed them before Holo could call out to him; a look of surprise crossed his face before he approached them with a smile and a wave.

"Now this is an interesting party."

Lawrence was clearly bewildered to see Tanya, but he quickly donned his mask of calm, like any seasoned merchant would.

"You haven't had too much to drink, have you, Holo?"

"What a fool you are."

Holo seemed displeased to see her husband, but she also looked like she was blushing. Lawrence, of course, only reacted with a slight grimace before removing his wallet from his hip and placing it straight on the table in front of them.

"I can leave this with you, because Miss Elsa's here."

Though this was his offer to pay for their drinks, Elsa was astonished by how smooth-tongued he was.

"Well, I wouldn't want to interrupt your delightful evening chat," he said, attempting to leave. It was his sheep's instinct that was telling him to go.

It was Holo the wolf who stopped him.

"We are drinking because we are talking about you."

"..."

Lawrence tried to flash a smile with his merchant's mask, but he could not quite pull it off because he sensed something was off with Holo.

"Well, um..."

"Sit," Holo commanded, and Tanya, who had been sitting beside her, hurriedly got up from her seat and rounded the table, cautiously settling back down beside Elsa. What wafted by her was a sweet, deep forest scent, unlike perfume, and Elsa finally understood why she had attracted so much male attention.

"Should I pray?"

Lawrence was clearly not expecting something fun out of this conversation, especially considering how Holo glumly brought her drink to her lips.

But Elsa could tell that Holo's sullen look was because she was considering how to broach the topic with Lawrence.

Not wanting to wait any longer, Elsa gave a short sigh and said, "Holo came to me with concerns that Salonia's bishop was up to no good."

Lawrence immediately understood that the first victim in this plot would be himself.

"Is this about the title?" Lawrence asked, and Holo looked away in a dramatic huff. "Is she thinking that…restless footing is more easily stolen away?"

This was doubtlessly an interaction that had repeated itself between the two since the day they met.

An obvious troubled smile crossed Lawrence's face, like the merchant he was, and he sighed.

"I have double—triple calculated the projected losses and gains, and I know that the bishop has his own motives."

"Fool," Holo spoke at last, turning wholly to face him. "Land? A noble name? That cannot come cheap. Do you plan on selling the bathhouse?"

She was a wolf avatar, once called the wisewolf—she had no interest in any renown the human world had to offer. While it might seem the case at first, this wolf whose love for meat and drinks over a banquet did not actually desire such things.

The reason Elsa scolded Holo like a child for her slovenly lifestyle was because there was nothing overly pompous about Holo that was worth mentioning, and there was a comfortable air between them as they both shared opinions on a great many things.

"Mister Lawrence, I do not think the bishop would propose an idea that would mainly benefit another. As frivolous and opportunistic as he seems, he is ruthless."

Though she typically hesitated in speaking ill of those with higher ranks in the Church, it was how she genuinely felt. Lawrence seemed to shrink away from the way Holo and Elsa looked at him, like a merchant being questioned at a checkpoint.

"Well, um… Do you mind if I give you an excuse?"

Elsa looked at Holo, and Holo sunk her canines into her grilled meat with displeasure.

"I am curious to hear what sort of flattery the bishop has been subjecting you to."

Lawrence gave a strained smile in response to what Elsa said and replied, "I will not pay a single silver myself."

"What?" Holo sputtered in disbelief.

"He proposed that, in exchange for receiving the title, the tariff levying powers that come with it, and the rights to land in the Salonia region, I pay a fixed sum to the Church every year."

"…"

Holo narrowed her eyes, looking at Lawrence in confusion, before turning to look at Elsa.

"I see," Elsa said. "That means he is not particularly attached to the privileges the Church has, so long as the amount of money going into his pocket is the same every year."

"Those titles are collecting dust somewhere in the church storehouse right now. It's not a loss for the bishop at all."

That meant no one's wallet would hurt in the exchange, and the bishop would earn a powerful ally in Lawrence. It was an easy-to-understand deal, one that the bishop would very likely propose.

But to Elsa, who had struggled with church ledgers throughout

126

the land with all the turmoil that surrounded the church now, felt a discomfort, one she was not fully satisfied with.

"If he were to propose this to me, I would then be motivated to keep tariffs high. I would have to pay him every year, you see. And even if the church decides to lower tariffs in the future, they will be still expect the same amount of money from me."

The whole debt crisis in town had started when the bishop hastily threw an merchant into jail over a debt, but he was shrewd when it came to these things. He was a true scoundrel. Elsa sighed.

"And so do you plan to take the bishop's side?"

When Elsa asked, Holo, who was not interested in the details but desperately wanted to know the short answer, turned to look at Lawrence as she bit into her new plate of meat. It was almost as though she was threatening to do the same to him if she did not like his answer.

"I'm a bit conflicted."

What surprised Elsa was that she had not been expecting such an evasive answer.

"Miss Tanya being here must mean…you three were looking into the origins of the tariffs, weren't you?"

Tanya, who had been sitting by her lonesome, not quite a part of the conversation, immediately perked up.

"A portion of the goods in this city have oddly high tariffs," Lawrence explained. "They say that stems from the Hero Voragine's work."

"He's the one who defeated the great serpent." Tanya gave her friendly smile, since she understood this conversation.

Lawrence smiled in response and continued, "That was a long time ago. And you know what they say—don't pour new wine into an old wineskin."

"…Do you mean that people doubt these origins?"

"No one likes taxes. Any strong allegation needs an equally strong excuse. Persuading people with a figure of myth who may or may not have actually existed can only go so far."

The shrewd bishop may have sensed that a shadow was being cast over the authority of an old tale.

He then set his mind into motion, trying to figure out a way to keep earning the same amount of money despite anticipating the lowered tariffs in the future.

And just as he had forced church work upon Elsa, he was dressing up a dying candle and trying to pass it off to Lawrence, assuring the merchant that the candle was all his, so long as it kept illuminating the church.

"With solid grounds for the tariffs, then I believe accepting the offer would not be a bad idea. But if it is indeed an entirely made-up story, then there is a very good chance that you would be losing out here, especially since the tariffs will indeed come down one day."

If tariff income went down despite having made the promise to pay a fixed fee each year, then whoever owned those interests would suffer huge losses. The deal offered to Lawrence was not without its disadvantages.

"'Tis as though we are meant to find this great serpent," Holo said to Lawrence with a disappointed look, her elbows planted firmly on the table either because she was drunk or vexed.

Lawrence then smiled at Holo before turning to Elsa.

"And God must have had a hand in this today, because there so happens to be a native from a village with a serpent myth right here."

Lawrence had mostly seen through the bishop's scheme.

And on top of that, he knew he had a lot of resources within his reach.

Hidden beneath their courteous smiles was a battle of wits between Lawrence and the bishop.

The winner would profit greatly, of course, but for Lawrence, it came with the extra prize of showing off to Holo.

Elsa turned to meet Holo's gaze, and she shrugged.

Holo threw back her wine cup to drown out her utterance, "You lot are unbelievable."

If the myth about the great serpent turned out to be true *and* they could provide solid proof of such, then it would be a powerful reason for them to keep tariffs as they were. But conversely, if the myth turned out to be nothing but a tall tale, then it would be very difficult for the town to maintain the historically high tariffs. That was the gist of the situation, but Elsa still had something she wanted to ask Lawrence.

The day after their conversation at the square, Salonia's grand market and the future festival were both entering their final stages. Their festival did not have venerable origins, unlike most other places, and instead was simply meant to celebrate the year's harvest, to have one last big party before the bleak winter, and to venerate a saint that had been retroactively created to fit the celebration, so it was essentially a big, ordinary feast.

Since Holo was the one who helped select the alcohol that would be served at the final ceremony, the townsfolk had roped her into helping prepare for the festival bright and early in the morning. She went to practice a quick ceremonial exchange and have adjustments made to the costume she would wear on the day.

The bishop, too, was in charge of running the festival, so he was absent from tariff meetings that day.

And so Elsa, who found Lawrence staring idly as the townsfolk prepared the stage for their revelry in the square from a nearby tavern, invited him into the church.

"What do you think of the tariffs?" she asked.

"What do I think, hmm?"

Lawrence gave her a very mercantile-like expression of feigned ignorance, then dropped his hammer on a walnut. They sat together in a corner of the church on the flagstone floor, splitting the walnuts Tanya had brought from her mountain as a souvenir.

"As a matter of justice," she elaborated.

"What do you mean?"

The walnut shells, after being roasted to the point where they just barely cracked open, were easily split with the hammers.

Lawrence picked out the inside of his walnut with delight, as though justice or truth itself had been hidden inside it.

"Tariffs pay for road repairs, waterwheels, city governance, and the guards who keep order. But not every coin collected by those tariffs goes toward those things," she said.

"Sometimes they also fill another's coffers. Like a botfly gorging itself on blood, right?"

Elsa brought down her hammer, cracking a walnut.

"This church does not need any more money. And cheaper lumber prices means that people can live in houses for less."

"And winter is coming up soon. People will need to light their hearths."

"And thus, justice."

Lawrence was not a completely heartless merchant, but that did not mean he was completely altruistic, either.

"I understand what you mean, Miss Elsa, but in the coming months without any farmwork, the villagers who dig up peat may want lumber prices to remain high."

Just as it was the farmers' job to carry the lumber to the peat-diggers' villages, the lumber trade belonged to the affluent merchants.

Once he brought up the line of thought that tariffs were on the people's side, then it was difficult to say which was which.

"But did you not say that the tariffs here are too high?"

Lawrence watched Tanya, who sat apart from them splitting walnuts with some of the other town girls, even as he did the same. The girls, seemingly bored of the task, were instead combing Tanya's fluffy hair, braiding it, and pulling it up as they pleased with giggles.

"It is, yes. Unnaturally so."

Elsa, who had lived in a small village and had worried a lot about the tax problem, considered taxes as something that made people suffer. Watching Lawrence work to preserve such high tariffs left an unpleasant taste in her mouth.

"Don't you think we should lower them, then?"

Unlike Holo, Lawrence was not the type to break from Elsa's gaze if the situation did not suit him. He stared back at her, then gave a slight smile.

"This town has its own history. This isn't something an outsider can so easily fiddle with."

He must have sensed the anger wafting from her—*How dare you look me in the eye and spout sophistry*—because he finally looked away.

"…Which is why I think we should learn their history."

He glanced over at Tanya and the girls before gazing up at the church's high ceiling. The women who then entered from outside brought them freshly baked bread. A delicious aroma filled the air; the women left the bread there, took some of the walnuts, then left. They had been baking bread since before sunup all to prepare for the festival the following day. While acorn bread was not something Elsa would willingly eat, she suspected bread with walnuts was rather nice.

"Do you believe that the great serpent actually exists?"

Lawrence's wife was a wolf.

When Elsa asked him that, instead of his merchant's smile, he offered her a real one.

"I actually want to rely on you because I think you'd be eager to help me out."

Tereo's guardian spirit had, in fact, been a snake.

"I serve the Church's god."

"Right."

Elsa was, of course, disappointed when he brushed her off with an emotionless response.

Though he seemed like nothing more than a boneheaded sheep when he was with Holo, he was much more like a slippery merchant when she dealt with him one-on-one like this.

"Miss Holo seems anxious that you're in such high spirits."

She could not, of course, tell him that Holo was feeling suffocated by his desire to show off, but perhaps they discussed it the night before.

Elsa could not tell either way through his merchant's demeanor, but at the very least, he could not deny what she said.

"I…can't deny that I'm in high spirits, no. This is a reward beyond my wildest dreams, you see."

He did not sound as though he was lying, and that frankly shocked Elsa.

"I did not know you wanted such things, too."

She could hardly picture him taking up the mantle of landlord, but Lawrence himself gave a bashful smile.

"I think you will find this silly, too, Miss Elsa."

"…How so?"

Lawrence cracked the walnut and picked out the insides.

"The Voragine family privileges come with considerable influence over land. That is what I'm after, if anything."

"…I don't understand."

Elsa could tell that he was not deliberately trying to obfuscate what he was saying, and that it was simply difficult to explain, but she still could not imagine what he meant. As she sat thinking, Lawrence continued, as though trying to divert the topic.

"Well, it's an overly optimistic calculation at this point, but you know what they say—the goddess of luck only has bangs."

"You must take the opportunity that presents itself?"

"Yes."

Lawrence tossed the walnut shell into the waste sack and wiped his hands.

As Elsa watched him, she could not help but ask, "But you said you are relying on me. Do you think I have special eyes that can see great serpents?"

Lawrence flashed a self-deprecating smile in response.

"Holo is very cranky. That's why I need your help to get things moving, Miss Elsa."

"Hmm?"

For a moment, Elsa did not know what Lawrence meant. Yet she noticed Lawrence's mischievous attitude, and finally understood what he was trying to tell her.

"If I am to help you, then does that mean Miss Holo must come along as well?"

"Wolves are very picky about territory, you see."

She could not believe this man.

He was desperate to show off to Holo, yet he was anxious that if he were to pursue the topic any further, she would get genuinely angry with him. Yet the only reason he could not bear to give up on his chase was not because he wanted to make a name for himself, but because he wanted to please his beloved wife.

As a member of the clergy, part of whose job was to preach love, she found it difficult to admonish him.

"You two have not changed one bit."

They were never direct; always thinking of each other in a roundabout way.

"I will take that as a compliment."

The way Lawrence said that brought a smile to Elsa's face as she brought down her hammer on the walnut with even more force.

Preparations for the festival must have ended in the morning as Holo came to the church a little after noon. Her cheeks were slightly flushed, likely because she had been treated to alcohol, but the reason her eyes seemed glassy was more likely that there had been trouble between her and Lawrence the night before.

Lawrence, who had tempered his merchant's audacity, easily pretended not to notice something was wrong with his wife and asked Elsa if she would be willing to accompany them to look into the legend of the serpent.

He made an exaggerated glance at Elsa and gave her a slight wink; Elsa emitted a sigh and agreed. Holo insisted she would go along as well, as though not wanting her own prey to be snatched away from her. Holo knew she was being roped into something.

In Elsa's eyes, their interaction was a clash of wily expectations, a childish stubbornness that used absolute faith in each other as a shield, and there was nothing noble about it.

And so, Elsa had been roped into their playful back-and-forth, yet she agreed to go along with it all because she felt responsible for being witness to their love.

Tanya came along, too, and they all hopped on a cart to the old Voragine territory in the Salonia area.

"It would make things much easier if they had the skull of the great serpent on display," Lawrence said, reins in hand.

Holo, who sat next to Lawrence, shawl draped over her shoulders and sobering up in the chilly autumn wind, said, "If such a thing existed, then it would have been installed in the church ages ago."

"I read over the annals again," Elsa interjected from her spot

136

in the cart bed with Tanya, saying, "and the way it was written could be interpreted that it was chased away, not so much killed."

It would be much more effective for the Church if they simply announced outright that they had killed it. Even if it had just been chased away.

But one could also look at it with a cynical eye and say that the true reason was because if such a claim spread far and wide, then people would begin to clamor for proof.

"Did it not escape to the mountain you live on?"

Holo glanced back at Tanya. The squirrel avatar, who had been playing with the braids the village girls had woven into her hair, sat up straight in surprise.

"N-no. I would have known if a large snake lived nearby."

The mountain in the Vallan Bishopric at the time had been rendered completely bare due to the mining operations, so everyone doubtlessly had a very good view of the area.

"Can such a beast be vanquished with human spears and swords anyway?" Holo mused.

If it was indeed a giant snake, then its scales must have been as hard as steel. It was hard to imagine that anything could have cut or pierced them.

Elsa pictured the script written in the annals, translated it into vernacular in her head, and said, "'The Hero Voragine brandished his blade and plunged it into the snake's neck. The snake raised its great head and gave a final cry. The plains of Salonia have known peace ever since...'"

Once she was finished with her little story, Holo scoffed.

"Perhaps it awoke from a nap because there was a tickle on its neck, and it simply yawned."

Elsa could easily imagine the same.

"If the snake had any ill will to begin with, Salonia would have been in grave danger. Nothing in the annals mentioned any damage to the city."

"There were likely horses and sheep tastier than humans here, and it was unlikely it missed a town in an area with such good visibility."

"There are many stories of pagan snake gods who adore alcohol in particular."

The priest who raised Elsa had been in the habit of collecting stories on the pagan gods. Elsa had collected similar stories of her own when she left home to travel and mentioned it as she flipped through her memory.

"Then does that mean 'tis not a made-up story?"

Holo knew that the bishop had carefully calculated this entire situation, so she was hesitant to allow her husband to get too deeply involved with it, which of course meant she was likely hoping that the story of the serpent was but a tall tale.

She turned a pointed gaze on Lawrence, but he only shrugged.

"A regular old warrior became a landowning noble overnight, and even gained the right to levy tariffs in a town that was still developing. It shouldn't be all that shallow. I think taking down a serpent of that caliber would certainly earn a reward that great, and conversely, I can't think of anything else that would explain what happened here."

Elsa nodded to herself in agreement. Lawrence was not simply elated by a prospect too good to be true; he was carefully evaluating what he had seen and heard, so that perhaps he could find the treasure if he chipped away at it.

But that was precisely why Elsa thought it strange.

Did Lawrence genuinely believe that the great serpent existed?

Considering his partner was a legendary wolf spirit, it was not odd to think that he would be more likely to believe in the possibility than most. On the flip side, however, that meant he was trying to obtain privileges that came about all because this great serpent, one of the old pagan gods, had been killed. Elsa thought him a bit insensitive as someone who made a wolf spirit his wife, given that she was not all that different from the serpent.

One could claim that wolves and snakes were not very similar, but there was something that did not sit right with her.

She had so many questions—it seemed so out of character for Lawrence to want to maintain high tariffs, to align himself with forces that opposed justice. She looked doubtfully at him, wondering what on earth this merchant in sheep's clothing was plotting, as the cart slowed and reached a rather lively spot on the road.

"What is this?" Holo asked, surprised. Perhaps she had never seen something like this before.

"A pontoon bridge," Lawrence explained. "Have you never been on one before?"

There were no proper bridges over the river to the east of Salonia. Instead there were several boats that spanned the water, wooden planks laid on top to connect one side to the other.

"Are we to cross here? There are boats beneath it! Why do they not build a bridge?!"

"I believe it's because the water levels change drastically across the seasons, such as when the snow melts," Elsa explained. "This is a far better idea than building a bridge."

Building a bridge that can withstand any water level took a considerable amount of time and money. With the constant threat of it being swept away due to seasonal changes, it made much more sense to build a pontoon bridge, which could be easily set up and dismantled. Elsa's own village had an unbelievable number of arguments over rebuilding the smallest bridges, too.

Those thoughts crossed Elsa's mind as she directed her gaze upstream, where she spotted a waterwheel attached to a boat in very much the same manner. Even if the water levels changed, the waterwheel on the ship could maintain the same distance from the water's surface, which made it more reliable. To a region that relied on threshed and milled wheat, a reliable waterwheel was a matter of life and death.

"Humans come up with the strangest things…"

Though despite this being a pontoon bridge, it had a lot of traffic, so it was much wider and preferable to a wooden bridge over a small stream that seemed on the verge of collapse. Merchants and villagers were presently crossing the very same pontoon bridge with full carts and no fear whatsoever.

But it was still over boats. The faint wobble of the water was likely a shock to the wolf within Holo.

Tanya the squirrel, who could easily clamber across trees, was more excited about crossing the river, and after Lawrence paid the crossing fare and glanced back at them, she took the initiative to walk ahead.

"We should go as well," Elsa said to Holo before adding, "I hope your steps are not unsteady from drinking."

"Fool!"

The wisewolf gingerly took a step forward, slowly walking down the middle of the pontoon bridge.

The river was rather wide, and plenty of other ships were coming and going.

But with the pontoon bridge blocking the way, that meant a canal had to be built beyond the sandbank where the bridge ended so that the ships could freely come and go.

"This is a nice river port."

"I've heard that this is where tariffs are collected for goods going downstream."

Lawrence, who had crossed the bridge slightly later than the rest, finally caught up and told them what he'd learned.

"And when there's a lot of snowmelt right before spring, they completely dismantle the bridge and send a lot of lumber downstream. It's apparently a safe place, so you don't get swept away by the lumber or the turbulent water."

"And so, no bridges."

It was not realistic for humans to carry heavy items like logs. The reason most large cities were by the river was because it was easier to bring in construction materials that way. And when bundles of massive logs, big enough for multiple people to ride on at once, came constantly rushing down the river in snowmelt, even the sturdiest of bridges would have a difficult time surviving.

They discussed this as they crossed the sandbanks, passed through a little hut where an official was stationed, then approached a small wooden bridge built over the canal. The river wall was fitted with a wooden frame, and small boats packed with grains were moored there. The opposite bank was lined with buildings—storehouses, taverns, and what looked like inns for sailors.

There were also several stalls plotted alongside the road that stretched out onto the plain, and delicious-smelling smoke wafted their way.

"Do you want something?" Lawrence asked Holo, who looked away in a huff out of pride, then quickly hopped back onto the driver's perch on the cart.

Lawrence gave a defeated smile, and his gaze met Elsa's, who offered a small smile in return. She helped Tanya up onto the cart bed as she struggled, and quickly followed suit.

"There are no trees here. It's so sad," Tanya suddenly remarked as they left the lively river bank.

"The fields are like sheared sheep at the end of the harvest."

The area around Salonia served as the city's breadbasket, with fields extending in every direction as far as the eye could see. The shrubs that divided the fields and lessened the severity of the wind that blew over them were scattered throughout, but that only made the scenery seem all the emptier.

Sacks of wheat that filled the ships on the river and the town's markets all came from these massive fields.

"I do not dislike the sight," Holo said as she sat on the driver's perch, a sleepy look crossing her face. It was in the middle of the harvest for these fields; there were girls with long, braided hair who were hacking away at the wheat with large scythes. Holo gazed upon the villages, delighting in their harvest with a kind eye.

As they proceeded forth along the gentle, unchanging road, Tanya started nodding off, and Elsa started to stifle her yawns.

Lawrence reached out to Holo, who had fallen asleep against him, and said, "Look, we can see it now."

His statement drew Elsa's gaze toward the front of the cart. And she could faintly make out a building sitting atop a small hill far ahead of them.

"That's the old Voragine castle. I heard they use it to store grain and as an assembly hall now, though."

"*Yaaawn... Hff.*"

Holo huffed—either because her nap had been interrupted, or because the topic itself displeased her—but Lawrence did not flinch.

"It seems to be a lovely stone building."

It even had a tower, which suggested that it may have even served as a fort in its heyday.

"I highly doubt that entire hill will serve as the snake's grave."

Things would go much quicker if the serpent was still sleeping there, and Elsa even considered asking it where Tereo's guardian might have gone if it were.

"…You could take it down, couldn't you, Lady Holo?"

Tanya sat huddled in her spot with great anxiety, but Holo gave a dauntless smile.

"Even if we cannot win, we simply need to run whilst it feasts on this foolish sheep."

Said foolish sheep guiding the horses drew his lips tight in a dry smile as he pressed them forward.

The wheat in this area had yet to be reaped; great, mature ears of the crop danced in the wind.

With a quiet, fond look, Holo gazed out over the waves of gold from atop her perch, and Elsa saw the kindness in Lawrence's eyes as he stole a look at her.

She needed nothing else to understand.

When she had asked him in the church as they split walnuts why he was so intent on pursuing this opportunity, Lawrence had faltered in his explanation.

He had looked so bashful when he did.

After a long series of twists and turns, the couple sitting on the driver's perch had made a home for themselves far to the north and opened a bathhouse. To Elsa, who had been born and raised in the plains, the place was so absurdly remote that she did not even think that "deep in the mountains" was an appropriate descriptor for the location.

While Holo had originally lived in a similar mountainous region, she had one day headed south on a journey south and found herself in a village where she governed the wheat harvest for centuries—a place that had wheat fields for as far as the eye could see, completely unlike the looming mountains of Nyohhira.

However, Elsa was convinced that Lawrence did not have the slightest intention of selling the bathhouse in Nyohhira, which Holo had been afraid of.

143

That was because this man was not unlike a gentleman in waiting who made every effort to make sure his princess was in the best of moods at a booze-filled get-together. And now he was trying to feed her sweet, sweet dessert after serving her fill of salty food.

"We're here," he said.

How much of Lawrence's innocence had Holo taken notice of?

There was no way for Elsa to know. But Holo leaped lightly from the driver's perch, took in a lungful of the wheat's sweet scent, and her thick-haired tail rustled beneath her clothes.

They could not see Salonia from atop the small hill.

Perhaps it would be visible from atop the tower, but one would pay no mind to it in daily life.

Living here, in a vantage point that gave clear view across one's entire realm, could certainly offer a taste of what it was like to rule.

"Oh? Miss Elsa?"

After knocking on the old Voragine gates, out came a familiar face—one of the assistant priests from Salonia's church. Though Elsa was technically a priest with no qualifiers in any manner, her position was still temporary, which meant that even the assistant priests in a church as big as Salonia's technically ranked above her in status. He had a mustache growing on his upper lip to give himself a more dignified, older appearance because he was hoping to climb the Church's ladder. This assistant priest, who would most certainly look very young without the notable facial hair, was surprised by their visit, yet welcomed them with open arms.

"Ah-ha, so you're mediating the tariff dispute."

The old Voragine castle looked like a giant stone box from far away, but after passing through the gates, they found a wide garden and the building itself set rather far back. There was an open wooden gazebo on the garden grounds, likely serving as a place for threshing wheat or storing it at the end of a harvest.

There was a quiet air about it, and no signs that anyone used this estate as their regular home.

As they cut across the garden, giving their reasons for visiting, the assistant priest gave an astonished laugh. "Well, that certainly sounds like something the bishop would come up with. Managing the fields and the hamlets is hard work. He must think he can push all of those responsibilities onto someone else."

Though the facade was made of stone, the inside of the first floor of the main house was made of packed dirt and was filled with the familiar scent of dust.

The main hall, where the lord would have situated himself, was now filled with a jumbled mix of bales of hay and farming tools; a thin dog, either belonging to the estate or simply a stray that had found its way inside, wandered about, gazed up at Holo with servile eyes.

The assistant priest guided them to a long table by the hearth and poured them all wine, which had been warmed too much after being left by the fire and had lost all its alcoholic content.

"Does wheat not turn much of a profit?"

The bishop seemed to mainly want to preserve the income that came from levying tariffs, and whatever other profits the fief generated would go straight into Lawrence's pocket. That meant the bishop had placed all the troubles that came with managing the land as well as the danger that tariff income would fall in the coming years on the scales, and ultimately decided that simply keeping the tariff income alone was the most beneficial move for him.

"I would say so. It's not a problem during years like this, when the harvest is good, but unfortunately, it comes in waves."

"Still, it isn't as though you can adjust wasted everyday expenses."

One of the responsibilities Elsa had been saddled with was to manage the Salonia church's ledgers. She had fought with numbers that could only be described as irresponsible, sloppy, incoherent—so when she interjected sharply, a grimace crossed the assistant priest's face.

"Precisely. Our expenses are the same as every year, yet it is relatively often that our income drops drastically, and it causes much confusion. Like three years ago—there was a fungal outbreak."

Elsa noticed that as Holo sipped her wine—which was decidedly not very good—her ears twitched under her kerchief, and she turned her gaze toward the assistant priest.

That was because this was the same disease that had proven a problem in the whole commotion surrounding Elsa's own town, Tereo. It was said that eating the wheat after it had gone black and sticky from the disease would cause people to hallucinate, and for those pregnant to miscarry.

Once even a small portion of the field started showing signs of disease, the entire field had to be put to the torch, and even the slightest rumor meant the land's entire harvest would sell poorly.

"That must have been horrible."

"Indeed, it was a trying time. Just remembering how the people swarmed us, asking for God's help brings pain to my heart."

It was the clergy's job to help alleviate the people's suffering, yet there was little doubt that the bishop had saddled his assistants with all of that responsibility, and he was hoping to avoid similar problems that might arise in the future by doing the same.

"And if not, then we were overwhelmed every day by other complications, such as maintaining the waterwheels for the mills, or land division. I suppose giving up the wheat income is a cheap price to pay if it means off-loading all of that onto someone else." The assistant priest laughed dryly; it was very likely he had been sent here by the bishop for the exact same reasons.

Even the most pastoral-looking farming villages were not so perfect on the inside.

"But in that case, there is still one question among all the nice things the tariff rights have to offer," Lawrence spoke, and everyone turned to look at him. "How did House Voragine end up with these tariff rights?"

The assistant priest sighed, his whiskers shuddering under his breath, and he shrugged. "The bishop summoned you because the lumber merchants were pressing him for answers on the same matter, didn't he?"

The Hero Voragine was said to have fought with a great serpent right in this area many years ago, after it had brought chaos to the region.

"Is the story of the great serpent being vanquished true?" Lawrence asked, feigning ignorance.

The assistant priest frowned, then said stiffly, "You must know of God."

Though he might not personally believe it to be real, if he mentioned that aloud, then the tariffs the church collected under the Voragine name would turn out to be a scam. He was not in a position to say precisely what he believed, so just as a clergyman from a big city would often do, he deftly avoided answering the question.

"Is there anything here that could still serve as proof?" Elsa asked.

The assistant priest immediately gave a shake of the head. It did not seem any great serpent skulls were left conveniently lying about.

"Would you mind if we took a look around the castle and the surrounding area?" Lawrence asked.

The assistant priest blinked, but could not think of any reason to say no. "Not at all. All documents regarding the territory rights

147

and privileges have been moved to the Salonia church for safe-keeping, but more complex records from the past should still be in the cellar. Ah, yes. Village mayors, other important individuals, and traveling merchants will be gathering here later. We will be talking about reaping and transporting the wheat, so it might be a nice opportunity to listen to what the locals have to say."

If Lawrence were to own this land, then this assistant priest would have no need to come all this way and mind the wheat, and he would undoubtedly start a longstanding relationship with the Salonia church. The assistant priest had made a sound judgment—if he were to assist Lawrence now and have Lawrence in his debt, then it would surely be an asset for when he climbed up the Church ladder in the future.

That was the first natural thought that came to Elsa's mind; when she realized that, she gave a quick shake of her head. Ever since leaving Tereo, she had taken on a much shrewder perspective of the clergy.

It was not uncommon for someone who was once honest and docile while living within their remote village to become much more distrustful and suspicious after returning from the city.

To make matters worse, that scared her; she rubbed her face with both hands and let out a tired sigh.

As the conversation entered a natural lull, the assistant priest stood up.

"Well, I need to go fetch people to help prepare for the meeting and for dinner, so you will have to excuse me for the time being. Feel free to look around the building. No one lives here and it's mostly used as storage, so nothing should be locked."

"Thank you."

The assistant priest bowed and vanished into another room.

"Well," Lawrence began, "I guess I'll go fight with the mold and the dust in the cellar."

"Hmph," Holo snorted and looked away. She was not upset by the situation; she simply did not like dust.

"She and I will look around to make sure the snake is not buried beneath us," Holo said while pointing meaningfully at Tanya. The squirrel stared blankly for a moment before nodding happily.

"Then Miss Elsa, could you look around the building and keep an eye out for anything that might speak to its history?"

It seemed obvious to Elsa that she would end up going into the cellar with Lawrence, but it was Lawrence himself who suggested this to her. Perhaps he did not want to subject her to the stench of mold and the layers of dust. Elsa was impressed by how considerate the merchant was when it came to these things.

At the same time, that only brought her an endless list of questions—why such a considerate man looked a fool whenever he stood next to Holo, for example.

"I hope to find something."

She looked between the easygoing duo, and all she could do was let her shoulders fall.

Holo took Tanya outside, and Lawrence rolled up his sleeves and ventured down the stairs. Elsa, not particularly enthused, began to take a look around the old fortress.

History was typically recorded on parchment, but it was at times painted onto the walls of buildings. That was how it been done at the chapel in the Vallan Bishopric, and as indecipherable as it seemed, the truth had lay hidden in there somewhere. Or perhaps there was a hidden shrine somewhere that worshipped the great serpent—that would speed things along quite nicely.

With those thoughts in mind, Elsa began to roam the building. All she found herself doing was confirming the existence of the vestiges of a familiar farming village life.

There was no furniture since no one lived here; heaps of straw sat idly in the corners of unused rooms. Carved candelabras, placed sporadically across the walls, had sat unused for a very long time; they were blanketed thick with dust.

The sights did not change very much as she moved up to the second and third floors. The only thing of note was the occasional large pot, much too big for family use; it had likely been used for festivals or other gatherings.

When she pried open the wooden shutters on a window, all she found was the view of the stone wall that encircled the garden. It did not offer a very good view.

Perhaps this place had once been subject to the fires of war if it served as a battlefield in the fight against the pagans.

Elsa pictured the massive serpent slithering about, acting as though the battle between humans was none of its concern, and she chuckled.

"Hero Voragine, did you truly vanquish the serpent?"

Trade had stagnated because of the serpent.

The building was firmly enclosed on all sides by stones and sharp angles, but if the serpent matched Holo's true size, then it could easily have destroyed the building by rubbing itself against the structure when it molted.

According to Church records, the hero had brandished his sword and plunged it into the serpent's neck.

Even if Hero Voragine was powerful enough to vanquish one of the pagan gods, Elsa knew, as someone who was familiar with a wolf known as the wisewolf, with a squirrel who tirelessly planted trees on a naked mountain, that there was more he could have done before stabbing it.

After all, it wasn't as though they were beings who couldn't be reasoned with.

She drew the window shut, and as she made her way down the stairs, an idea suddenly came to her.

"Perhaps...they were the same as this wolf couple."

When the possibility dawned on her, she found herself rather surprised. If the snake spirit and Hero Voragine reached an intimate understanding, then creating miracles was an easy ask.

"I believe Mister Lawrence anticipated this."

As one who had seen the wisewolf Holo's true form, Elsa was convinced that no human could face those sorts of beings and win by means of raw power alone. Lawrence, who had been with her for many more years, knew this even better than she did.

Coming up with the sort of situation that would lead to the highest probability of such a thing happening was not difficult.

The great serpent and the Hero Voragine were either lovers or friends, and thus the myth of this land was born.

"...I believe it's entirely possible we've heard a similar story in town before."

The man only seemed a fool when he was with his beloved wife—in any other setting, he was quite sharp.

And if the story of the Hero Voragine vanquishing the serpent was indeed a made-up one, then it made perfect sense why Lawrence would look into obtaining land privileges with a straight face.

In fact, if he could show Holo that there were others like them, then it would be good news for the gloomy wolf.

"But..." As Elsa exited into the garden she crossed her arms, walking beneath the sky as it took on the bright colors of sunset. "Mister Lawrence and the others confirming this fact and talking down the lumber merchants are two separate matters entirely. I wonder how he plans on approaching the regular townsfolk."

The problem was that their realization of the truth would not be enough. They would have to tell the lumber merchants of the serpent myth, and then convince them that the tariffs were just. And if something easy to comprehend, like a skull, was a simple matter to obtain, then the bishop would have already placated the merchants on his own.

That meant Lawrence would have to find some other decisive piece of evidence, but it was almost impossible to imagine what that could be, and the man himself showed no sign of knowing what it was, either.

What could Lawrence be chasing?

Or perhaps he had only convinced himself that he already had it?

"He does not have Miss Holo helping him, so it's unlikely he's using any special methods."

Elsa was the type of person who loved it when the logic involved was straightforward, when the lines of reasoning were perfectly straight, so she always found herself bothered when things were not perfectly and easily explainable.

As she walked around, she kept her eyes fixed on her feet while her head swam in thought; and eventually, she found herself outside the fortress.

Back in Tereo, whenever she looked up after doing that, she always found her husband with their children in tow, looking at her with a tired smile.

But in the Salonia plains, far from her village, all she found was a lone girl, sitting by herself in the autumn grasses.

Elsa approached Holo, recalling what it was like to hold a child's warm hand in her own.

"How are the wheat fields here?"

Holo did not even glance in Elsa's direction, though she stood right next to her, but her wolf ears, now out in the open due to the lack of people, flicked in response.

"I believe Mister Lawrence wanted you to see this view."

Stretching out endlessly before them was a sea of gold.

Elsa, who had been born on the plains, loved places like this far more than the cramped mountains of Nyohhira.

"Why not show him your appreciation?" she asked, and only refrained from adding, *in an innocent manner*, because she knew it might only sound contrary.

"Fool," Holo said curtly, but there was no force in her words.

Even the way her tail thumped against the grass was limp.

As Elsa stood beside her in silence, Holo eventually gave a big sigh.

"I am delighted he is trying to leave me things to remember him by," she said, resting her chin on her propped knee. She looked like a sulking child as she gazed out across the wheat fields. "But there are too many."

For a moment, Elsa thought about how privileged she was to have such a problem, but she recalled what the assistant priest said.

"Because it would be too much to handle them all, is that right?"

"Indeed. What a fool he is." She dropped her knees and folded her legs under her. "Perhaps he thinks I can create a good crop of wheat with a single flick of my tail."

"Can you not?" Elsa asked.

Holo finally turned to look up at her with a glare. "Of course I can."

"Then—" Elsa began, but stopped. That was not the only problem here.

In the decades to come, this young girl would see to the harvest, and then return home to her fortress to find herself alone. A good harvest would not bring her companion back.

While that was what Elsa was thinking, the words that actually came out of Holo's mouth were much more realistic than that.

"The care for wheat does not stop at its harvest. Like how humans grow tired from running, the ground, too, grows tired from growing. The fertile earth runs from the soil after a heavy rain, and canals often break. Those things are out of my control. Droughts, especially. And I am absolutely powerless once the wheat has been harvested. I cannot handle everything—I cannot ensure that the wheat will be sold at a proper price. I cannot promise that I will not be taken advantage of by blackhearted merchants. Human society is complicated, and quite a bother altogether."

The wisewolf understood that growing the wheat and managing a field were two entirely separate matters.

"We cannot leave our bathhouse empty. I am loathe to admit that I am much like my unworthy daughter—complicated matters, such as running a bathhouse, are beyond me."

People were calling their only daughter, Myuri, a saint, but it seemed that she was different from what the rumors said of her. What sort of girl was the daughter of Lawrence and Holo like?

When Elsa tried to picture her, she caught herself smiling. Surely, she was a dazzling, carefree girl.

And so, Elsa decided to speak her mind.

"It's a wonderful thing to be worried about..." She could feel Holo's dubious gaze on her, but she looked out to the fields with a smile before finally turning to face her. "...Am I wrong?"

Holo's hair, so close in color to the wheat that Elsa would surely lose sight of her if she waded through the fields, swayed in the wind as she pouted.

"No," she sighed deeply. "'Tis like alcohol and a hangover."

"All things in moderation."

"Precisely!" she cried, throwing herself onto the ground. "'Tis painful to be loved too much."

She showed no bashfulness nor any affectation—Elsa believed that she truly was loved too much.

And that was what made her smile just by being close to them.

"Would things not proceed more favorably if you left them in Miss Tanya's hands? No..." Elsa suggested, but quickly corrected herself. "She is much too kind. I doubt it would go over well."

"Aye. She is most suited to deal with trees in the mountains. Look how nervous she is when she is in an open space."

Holo sat up and jerked her chin in a direction; there was Tanya, taking small, uncertain steps, not unlike a lost child.

When she realized Holo and Elsa were watching her, her face lit up and she waved to them with both hands.

"I suppose that means the serpent is not here," Elsa said as she waved in return.

"No. I doubt it is no different from the distant past."

Tanya the squirrel rushed over to them and started shaking her head before either of the other two could ask. Holo praised her as she lent a hand to help the wolf stand.

"What on earth could that fool be plotting?"

They all knew that it would be very difficult for Lawrence to find any superhuman clues without Holo's eager help. And even if she did lend him a hand, it was unlikely the merchants could be convinced without hard evidence.

And since Holo herself knew that well, she had come to the same question as Elsa—though the chances of the snake existing were slim, if it had indeed lived, then how were they going to prove such a thing?

"We may learn something if we ask the locals."

"Mm..." Holo placed her kerchief back over her head and hid her tail under her clothes. "The fool's fervor aside, 'tis a disgrace for the wisewolf not to see through his intentions."

To Elsa, this sounded less like a competition and more like a grievance that she was unable to see the same sights as he did, even though she was right next to him.

This wolf wanted to stay close to her companion, and gaze upon the same things, breathe the same air, and spend their time together forever.

It was hard to imagine that the sharp Lawrence had not noticed such a thing, but in truth, they had fallen out of step with each other.

Holo turned to Tanya to pick out the hay from her fluffy hair like a disgruntled sister. The amiable Tanya was simply happy to let her do so.

As Elsa watched, she felt like she had been brought back to a time when she was a younger girl, when she first met Holo and Lawrence.

Though it struck her as odd to think about it after all these years, she mused about how Holo had this odd aura about her that could create such an innocent atmosphere.

Elsa gave a small sigh with a self-deprecating smile, and she, too, reached for Tanya's hair. She undid the messy braids the girls from the church had put in her hair and re-braided them in a much neater fashion.

Holo was impressed by her skill, and Tanya stood there, delighted.

As Elsa indulged in feeling like a young girl again, Holo suddenly lifted her head and stared into space.

"Hmm?"

Holo's eyes darted across the scenery, eventually settling on the fortress entrance.

A frown immediately crossed her face.

"Why that face…?"

The spite in her tone was perhaps brought on by the sudden appearance of a boorish man among the three girls. Lawrence was waving at them, a piece of paper in his hand, and a terribly gleeful smile on his face.

From the perspective of the one who decided to make him her life partner, all she saw was a boyish innocence that would force her to be the adult in the situation, and sigh with unease.

Holo stood at the front with Elsa and Tanya behind her and they all made their way to Lawrence. The former merchant, who had often been called a foolish sheep, held a sheet of paper aloft with pride.

"I found our evidence."

"..."

Holo gave no response and instead snatched the paper from his hand.

Both Tanya and Elsa peered over opposite shoulders to see that it was a rather old map.

"What is this? Do you mean to say you found a map revealing where the snake went?"

It was just an old map, and even if there was any writing to suggest the serpent had passed through any particular area, the only ones who would believe it were small children who enjoyed fantasy.

Despite the doubtful looks of three women, he gave a bold nod without so much as a flinch.

"I'm going to show you proof."

"Hmm? D-dear, you—"

Holo grew flustered because she stumbled as Lawrence grabbed her hand and pulled her away.

She remained bewildered as he led her, glancing back at Elsa and Tanya. Holo looked just like a flustered girl who had been gossiping about someone she liked, only for the person in question to come along and suddenly drag her away.

"...What should we do?" Tanya asked, lacing her fingers

together in thought. The look on her face showed that she was not so much worried about Holo but was desperately curious to see what was going to happen.

Elsa did not have any close female friends her age back in Tereo, so all she had was her imagination—and she believed that regular girls, in this situation, would follow after them.

"Let's go."

Tanya nodded with delight, and Elsa led the way.

She, of course, was genuinely curious as to what it was that Lawrence discovered. In all honesty, however, she was more curious to know what sort of sentimental sight he was going to show Holo, considering the elation on his face as he dragged behind him the bewildered wisewolf.

That, too, made her a lot like a young girl wanting to see her friend's romance play out.

"O-oh, my. What should we do?" Tanya, who had been running like she was chasing acorns as they rolled down the mountainside, suddenly came to a stop, pressing her hand over her mouth as she spoke. "Is this their new den?"

For a moment, Elsa did not understand what she meant, but she eventually recalled that Tanya was a squirrel.

Lawrence had dragged Holo into the stone tower.

Perhaps the tower looked like a nest to the avatar of a tree squirrel.

After a moment's thought, Elsa said teasingly, "We must look and see whether or not this is a suitable abode for Miss Holo."

Tanya blinked her big, round eyes, then finally gave a carefree smile. "Of course!"

Elsa mused at how Tanya was a surprisingly naughty person as she opened the door Lawrence and Holo passed through not moments earlier and stepped inside the tower.

A spiral staircase led upward, and it was rather obvious that it had been built for greater reasons than for nobility to show off. Though when Elsa thought about how it would have been used in times of war, something about it struck her as strange. How useful would a single tower like this be in war if it sat alone in the middle of such extensive plains?

She found herself thinking about the pontoon bridge near Salonia. Things took on their forms for one reason or another, and the view at the top of a hill was enough to make anyone feel like they were a sovereign gazing out over their land.

Or perhaps there was something for which they had been keeping watch that required an even higher vantage point?

Or perhaps that was the snake?

Various thoughts crossed Elsa's mind as she climbed the stairs after Tanya.

With all those possibilities in her mind, she saw how the scenery out of the little windows in the wall grew more and more distant. She glanced around, hoping to find a painting that might detail the history somewhere; as they passed the third-floor window that looked down over the garden, they at last began to see the rooves of the buildings.

That was when she spotted the assistant priest walking through the courtyard with others. They seemed so small, like they belonged in a distant world.

The tower stairs continued upward.

Tanya's steps grew heavy as she ran out of breath, so Elsa encouraged her as they went up.

And just as she started to get dizzy, they exited out onto a place higher than the stone wall.

Another full round up the spiral staircase would take them to the top of the tower.

Elsa stopped not because Tanya was exhausted, or because they would run into Lawrence and Holo at the top of the tower.

It was because her eyes were fixed on the sight that greeted her beyond the window in the wall.

"No... Could this be...?"

She could not help but voice her thoughts; she gulped between ragged breaths and stared hard at what she saw.

As a servant of God, she told people of the divine miracles detailed in the scripture to cultivate their faith. On the other hand, she had taken in her father's footsteps to collect her own stories about the pagan gods. And then, the miraculous pair of the traveling merchant and the girl came to her town.

In her eyes, they lived in a fantastic world, and they showed her a side of the world she had not thought of before. And once again, they were doing the same thing.

Here they were showing her inviolable proof of a myth out of time.

"What? What?! Are those snake tracks?!"

Tanya came up right beside Elsa to peek through the hole in the wall and raised her own voice in shock.

There was no mistaking the sight—anyone would look at it and think the same thing.

Before them, in the golden fields of wheat as the grains bowed in the wind, illuminated in the autumn afternoon sun, was a distinct trail that could have only been left by a giant serpent.

"B-but, this..."

Elsa felt terribly confused by what she saw before her.

The easiest thing to confirm was with Tanya.

"Miss Tanya. Didn't you say there was no snake?"

Tanya gasped at the question. "O-oh, yes, you're right. But... huh? Then why...?"

Elsa doubted that Holo with her wolf's nose would have missed the presence of a snake. Or perhaps the serpent that left the tracks on the field was a being even greater than the likes of Holo or Tanya.

Something that could not be seen or sensed, but left trails like this on the wheat fields only.

Impossible, Elsa thought. And just as she did, a similar sentiment came from above.

"H-how could I have missed this?! 'Tis impossible!"

It sounded as though Holo did not quite understand what she was seeing, either. Her bewildered cry, which was almost a yell, caused Elsa and Tanya to exchange glances; Elsa brought a finger to her lips, then gestured for the both of them to venture up the stairs quietly.

"This snake…left a trail in the wheat…"

Elsa and Tanya came to a stop just as they were about to reach the top.

"Weird, isn't it? It's so hard to see when you're on the ground, but it's so obvious when you're up high."

They could hear the hint of pride in Lawrence's voice. Elsa could easily imagine Holo squaring her shoulders and puffing out her tail.

"Hrrgh… I do not understand, then. I sensed no snake at all. And most importantly—!" Holo's voice was pained, as though she were shaking off a nightmare. "The wheat would be bent, flattened entirely if there were a big snake slithering about atop it. Do you mean to tell me this snake was fluffy like mist, one that would be nice to pet?!"

Though Holo and her kind were unbelievable supernatural beings to regular humans, she was still confused and agitated. But her response came from a former merchant whose voice was calm, almost suppressing a laugh.

"It's the other way around."

"What?!"

"It wasn't slithering on top of the wheat. It was going under. And it's probably the same, in a way, even now."

"—!"

All Elsa could hear were Holo's fevered breaths. Words were failing her.

Holo likely stood perfectly still, her eyes wide, fangs bared, ready to leap forward at any moment.

But Elsa was in the same state of mind. She had completely forgotten about feeling like a young girl trying to eavesdrop on a love confession, and instead strained her ears to hear Lawrence's explanation.

"That isn't the great serpent, though."

"What?!"

"Wh-whoa, hey! Don't push me! I'll fall!"

Elsa could hear Lawrence panic as Holo rushed Lawrence, finally out of patience.

"It is *not* the serpent...? Dear... Dear, are you bli—oh. Hmm?"

It finally dawned on Holo as she held Lawrence in her grip.

Elsa could picture it so easily, as though she were there with them. Lawrence had been holding that old map in his hands.

She was astonished.

"Exactly. It's what's left of a river." His voice was gentle, as though he was carefully guiding her through his thought process. "There was an old topographical map of the area along with some other old maps. And this is an exact match with what we see here."

Tanya fidgeted, wanting to look out the window again, so Elsa moved over to give her room; she watched as Tanya scooted past her down the stairs, and she concentrated on the voices above her at the same time.

"This old river flows across the Salonia plain from the eastern mountain range to the southwest. And see, if you follow the snake tracks the entire way, you'd get to the mountains in the east, right? Then, you'll start getting very close to the river that we crossed if you go farther upstream."

Elsa could picture Holo turning to look where Lawrence was pointing, then turning back to look at him in disappointment.

There came a loud rustling of clothes and irritable footsteps.

"According to this map, there used to be two rivers cutting across the plain. The remains in the field are of the ones that dried up."

"B-but…"

Holo fell silent, and Elsa empathized with her bewilderment.

Holo had stood before that wheat field not long ago, after all.

Would she not have noticed if the flow of the old river left a physical mark on the land, an indent in the very ground? And most importantly, anyone who knew anything about minding wheat fields would question if it would remain unchanged, even after months and years of tilling.

And yet it was strange that an old river had left such a clear mark on the ground, like a carpet for the wheat. It was as though only the wheat itself knew how the land changed… When that thought crossed Elsa's mind, she almost exclaimed, but stopped herself.

Then wisewolf Holo arrived at the same answer.

"Drainage!"

"Very perceptive. I asked the villagers, and they said that the dirt was deepest only where the river used to be, which meant the plants there grew in a slightly different manner."

The ground where the river once was would have been filled with stones and pebbles. It was not realistic to manually remove all of that, so they made their fields by filling the depressions with soil. That would not affect the area in general, but it could never have the same sort of earth as its surroundings.

"It isn't enough to change the wheat harvest for better or worse, but the heights and stalks were slightly, but surely different. And so the only time you can see this is when the wheat is ripe and from high spots. We were lucky," Lawrence, very likely looking out over the fields, said, his tone relaxed.

"In which case...what of the snake?"

Elsa understood Holo's confusion, too. Because if the great serpent of myth was indeed the remains of this old river, then she would have to readjust her thought process in order to comprehend what this all meant.

What of the tale of the Hero Voragine, then? It was unlikely that his only achievement had been to notice the slight color difference in the wheat fields, hurriedly construct a tower, then claim a serpent once roamed there. Would such a thing even earn him tariff-levying privileges, or any titles at all?

Lawrence, of course, could explain it all, which was why he had brought Holo here with that big smile of his.

"The serpent that hampered trade did actually exist."

"..."

Lawrence had just told her that the mark on the field was not from the snake. Elsa could clearly sense Holo's bewilderment through her silence. Lawrence enjoyed leading her by the nose, especially since she typically had the upper hand between them, but he knew clear well what would happen if he got carried away.

He spoke to soothe her, but his voice still had a chuckle in it.

"It's pretty complicated."

"...Hmph."

Elsa could practically see Lawrence grimacing as Holo pouted.

"First, the Hero Voragine didn't actually kill a serpent. But he *did* take down something a lot like it."

It was wholly a riddle, and Holo the Wisewolf was cross enough to have absolutely no intention of waiting for an answer. Elsa could hear a gentle smile in Lawrence's voice, like he thought it was funny, as he continued talking.

"He killed the serpent not with a sword, but with a spade. He dried up the river."

Elsa took a step down the stairs, listening to Lawrence as she joined Tanya in looking out the window over the fields.

"But it'd be strange if anyone could become a noble by drying up a river, wouldn't it?"

Holo's tone in response was reluctant; perhaps she felt guilty for ignoring him any further. "Those who grew the wheat would only come to loathe him."

"Exactly. And you can't just make the snake a metaphor for the river. You remember how we crossed the pontoon bridge, right?"

"Aye, I do. What of it?"

"You asked why they didn't just build a big bridge over the river, remember?"

Elsa was a few moments away from answering the riddle herself, but the wisewolf let her wisdom be known.

"Because of all the lumber that comes down from the mounta—Oh!"

"Exactly. They float all the logs down the river. Imagine what it'd look like if you stood next to the river and watched them go by."

It would look like a massive snake.

"B-but, ah…"

"That's only half the story, though."

Even Elsa could picture Lawrence's exaggerated movements as he became more absorbed in the story.

"The river used to have two branches, remember? One of them never went to Salonia; it came this way. There are no towns out on these plains, and it's far out of sight."

Though Holo was a spirit from a bygone era, she had been traveling with this former merchant for a while now, and she had learned how to view the world the way he did.

"Smuggling."

As kind as Lawrence seemed, he was still a merchant at heart. Their journey together had not been entirely wholesome, and Holo had been exposed to much of the darkness of the mercantile world.

"There were plenty of people who decided to use this river for their lumber in order to avoid tariffs. Now, they couldn't do this out in the open, so they floated the lumber down the river at night. But just setting lumber free down the river meant the wood could get caught on tight corners. And so, they tied the thin pieces of lumber together to form what looked like rafts, and then people would stand at the front to guide it. And what do you need if you're doing this at nighttime?"

The moonlight could only provide so much light.

Using torches at the front of this dark procession could only make it look like one thing.

"It would look like…snake eyes in the dark."

"And it was the Hero Voragine who vanquished the serpent."

All by drying up the river.

"I had a rough idea of what happened when I saw the map in the village. I also thought it was very odd that the lumber merchants and the Church couldn't settle this ongoing dispute of theirs. I think everyone knows about this."

A keen-eyed passerby noticing a flaw in a long-held belief, especially one that had avoided scrutiny by locals for generations, was something that happened often in adventure tales, but not so much so in real life. The truth was so obvious that they could not put it into simple words.

The Church, at the time, had been busy fighting the pagans, so it had been much more convenient to dress it up as the story of a great serpent being killed; the lumber merchants were beholden to the immoral acts with which their predecessors sullied their hands.

Neither of them could say anything decisive, however, and remained in silent deadlocked stares when a traveler with a lot of sway but ignorance in local affairs came to town.

And so, they had called on Lawrence, hoping he would give them the advantage without him ever noticing the truth.

"But I'm not going to let them pull my strings like that."

Elsa could picture the smug look on Lawrence's face, and she could just as easily see the mixture of exasperation, vexation, and even joy on Holo's.

She could just scarcely hear Holo's tail, fluffed in displeasure, swishing back and forth.

"And I think this out-of-place tower was meant to serve as a lookout for smugglers who used the old river. Remember how Miss Tanya said that she heard merchants complaining about the snake that made it impossible to sell any metal from the mines? All the smuggling had likely caused control to become so strict that it affected legal trade."

Elsa understood—and it was because the Hero Voragine resolved this problem that he was awarded with tariff rights and a title of nobility out of it.

"That's more or less the myth of the great serpent of the Salonia plain."

When Elsa would stay the night at an inn while she was on the road, she had often encountered travelers sitting around the hearth in the great hall, ale in hand, sharing interesting stories of things they had encountered on their travels.

Lawrence had surely done the same almost every night when he was traveling with Holo.

When his familiar storytelling cadence came to an end, Holo had calmed significantly after being led so ruthlessly by the nose.

"You are honestly—"

"—Amazing, I know."

He had told the story in an amusing yet confident manner.

And, of course, it was not as though Holo genuinely thought Lawrence to be a foolish sheep.

It was because she could occasionally corner him in an argument, as he did to her, that Holo the wolf could not tear herself away from Lawrence.

"I suppose so, yes. Then what are you going to do?"

Elsa thought about how indifferent Holo sounded for only a brief moment.

She could tell from the footsteps above that Holo had drawn closer to Lawrence, perhaps holding his hand.

"Do you intend to obtain this field for yourself and then present it to me? The truth of this situation must be quite delicate for the Church."

She sounded like a wolf playfully nuzzling and nipping at her prey.

"If all know the truth, but none choose to divulge, it becomes impossible to pick a side."

She was right. If Lawrence were to side with the Church and obtain tariff and lordship rights and maintain high tariffs on the lumber merchants, then they would have to acknowledge that they were being punished for the wrongdoings of the past and may even be forced to admit the truth of the great serpent, that the legend fabricated by the church was exactly that—fabricated.

Lawrence replied in an almost casual tone, "Aww. I just have to be just friendly enough with both sides, don't I?"

"...Hrm?"

"I'll tell the lumber merchants that because of the wrongdoing their predecessors caused, they have no hope of ever having tariffs significantly lowered. But I'll tell the church that this myth they've been spreading is an outright lie, and that the people who were engaging in all the smuggling went to their graves years ago, and then propose they find a compromise with the merchants."

"...Mm."

"All I need from the lumber merchants is a little thank-you. And we can drink all we want with that money."

Holo's tail was probably already swishing when she heard of such an obvious reward.

"But...what of the field? Will you be giving up on it?"

Despite how hesitant she had been when Lawrence first brought it up, she seemed sad now that it was about to vanish from her grasp. Lawrence did not reply to her question right away.

Though he seemed foolish at a glance, the man was prudent; it was as though he was gently gifting her a treasure.

"Instead of thanks from the Church, I'm going to ask they send a set amount of wheat to Nyohhira each year."

"...You what?"

"Then, every year, when we bake our bread using that wheat, we'll remember what happened today."

Ale had no value once consumed, and coins were little more than useless baubles.

But receiving wheat every year, harvested from land rich with memories, was a different story.

Holo spent her days writing every detail of her activities down. She had been frightened when she saw her partner's face illuminated by the light of an inn that was not her bathhouse, her home. Each new line served as a reminder that time flowed differently for the two of them. Even the mightiest of rivers would eventually run dry.

One day, her words might also dry up.

But wheat, with its myriad flavors and aromas, could create fresh memories.

"If the wheat's not good, then just have Myuri come check up

170

on things. Or you can come yourself. Might not be a bad way to spend your time, you know, coming down here a—"

Elsa decided not to think about why Lawrence did not finish his sentence.

Tanya strained her ears curiously and she even began to crane her neck in an attempt to see them, but even the straitlaced Elsa knew that lingering here any longer would be tactless of them. She placed her hand on Tanya's shoulder and pointed down the stairs with a smile.

Elsa's heart was full as they made their way down the stairs.

From Tereo, she had walked to church after church, hoping to be of some use to the clergy as it floundered in the torrent of the ages. What she had seen over and over again were the devout acting in ways unbefitting servants of God, though there may have not been any malice behind their actions.

Anything truly genuine was a rare find in this world. People often painted things in brighter hues; they often dressed them up to seem greater than they were.

But at times, she did come across things like *this*.

Once they exited the narrow tower staircase and came to the open garden, Tanya heaved a deep sigh.

Elsa turned her gaze up to the top of the tower and could not help the smile tugging at her lips.

The smile was not just because of the deep affection the couple had for each other, but because of the way she herself felt.

"It's been quite a while since I've felt homesick."

Her home was full of noise, with things constantly happening, and her memories consisted almost entirely of her yelling.

But that was where she truly belonged.

Perhaps it was nowhere near as saccharine as Lawrence and Holo's relationship, but her family was still precious to her— blankets had to be readjusted after being kicked off in the night.

171

"..."

But that was when she noticed how still Tanya stood next to her. Though she would not point it out herself, Elsa saw envy, and a pronounced sadness, in Tanya's expression.

This squirrel spirit had spent many years alone in the mountains. Once, she had grown close to a traveler who had been passing through the area and ended up spending some time with them. She was still awaiting their return.

When she finally realized Elsa was staring at her, a guilty look crossed her face. So, without a word, Elsa pulled Tanya in for a hug, and they remained there for a long while before Elsa finally spoke up.

"My home is a bit far from here, but would you like to come with me?"

Tanya blinked, her lips mouthing words that never came.

The corner of Elsa's mouth turned upward in a teasing smile, and she pointed to the top of the tower.

"I believe you have the right to follow that happy-go-lucky couple, too, if you wanted to."

Tanya followed suit and also looked up, and by the time she looked back at Elsa, a warm look had crossed her face.

"Yes! I would love to go with you!"

There was no reason for Tanya to be left by herself on her mountain.

Elsa nodded, smiling, and added after a moment of hesitation, "Perhaps you may meet someone nice along the way."

Tanya's eyes widened and her face went red; she brought both her hands up to her cheeks. "But, the master..."

She was talking about the alchemist, the one who was likely dead by now. She might have had an inkling of what had become of him, but it was best not to dwell on it.

"But the master is too good for me, so I could never... So then, umm..."

She was clearly enjoying this.

Elsa smiled, gave a short laugh and said, "I, too, am still a child for enjoying talk of romance."

It was what it was.

Tanya beamed.

"There's so much I want to talk about!"

"Of course."

Elsa wondered if it was worth extending the conversation invite to the wolf.

She was likely the happiest girl in this world, and would have many unbelievable stories to share.

"We're going back to town!" Elsa called up to the top of the tower, planting her hands on her hips.

She would go home, too.

And when she pictured herself turning down any further work from that greedy bishop, she felt quite refreshed.

THE
COLOR OF
DAWN AND
WOLF

Back when Lawrence had yet to sprout a single hair on his chin, a traveling merchant came to his village. He became close with the man, and they left the village together.

His master had been an eccentric person, and though he had not taught Lawrence every trick of the trade, nor had he been a particularly kind benefactor, the treatment Lawrence received had not been as horrible as what the errand boys in large companies endured.

When he thought back on it, he likened the relationship to a stray cat taking in a puppy and raising it entirely on a whim. And the reason his mentor had been so strange was because his outlook on life was unique, formed after years of living on the road.

As he grew older than his mentor was at the time, Lawrence had now found himself gazing out over the autumn festival in Salonia, a town he had so happened to stop by in his first journey in a long while. It was strange how those memories suddenly came back to him.

From his window at the inn, he watched over the plaza; he watched as the people built a large stage, as the important folk from both the city and the church held some sort of celebration, and how the people reveled in one last party before winter came.

Salonia had no stand-out religious events, so the highlight of the autumn festival was the drinking contest, where people competed to see who could drink the largest amount of the distilled spirit made from the local wheat. He could hear them call out different names, and the most muscular dock boys from the river port and the most confident young clergy from the church came to the stage. It was, all in all, a very relaxed atmosphere.

As Lawrence looked down at the plaza, he found himself smiling because he spotted among them one small girl.

Her hair, colored in a way that would make her impossible to find if she were to slip in among the wheat fields, was braided today, which was unusual. Her petite stature and slender frame made her seem like a highborn lady, but the way she carried herself made her seem more imposing than anything else.

Sitting by the window, he smiled and thought: *There's the wolf.*

On the outside of the plaza, grilled sausages and freshly baked bread—and no alcohol—were being handed out to the spectators, and it was turning out to be a party full of song and revelry. As Lawrence watched Holo knocking back drinks right in the center of it all, he planned their journey to come.

The reason his mind went to his mentor, someone he had not thought about for a very long time, was because the thoughts had happened to spill forth after he opened his mental drawer of travel memories. Or perhaps because he had been rifling through that very drawer for a clue.

As he made his plans for their journey, there was something he needed to think about.

Along one's travels, a person would likely experience more

than joyous occasions. That was still the case when they were allowed to spend their time freely in such a lively city, too, as odd as it sounded. Perhaps the more enjoyable something was, the more pain it could potentially produce.

That was because a life on the road meant trading certainty and routine for flexibility—and stability for freedom.

"Once the festival is over, I believe I will be returning home."

It was yesterday that the priestess Elsa, the one who had spent quite a lot of time with them as of late, brought up the topic. It happened after they convinced the church and the lumber merchants to come to a compromise over the Salonia tariffs and were on their way back to their lodgings.

Holo had no interest at all in the tariff meetings, so she had gone ahead to the taverns at the town square, leaving Lawrence and Elsa to walk back together. Lawrence understood that she had been waiting for a moment like that to bring up their parting, but there was one thing he still didn't understand.

"Why not tell Holo first?"

Unbeknownst to him, Holo had come to speak with Elsa while he was occupied with the tariffs. Even when he watched Elsa scold Holo, and how Holo would ignore her, he noticed a closeness between them that he had not seen before.

And so he wondered why the conscientious Elsa did not tell Holo about this beforehand.

It was that thought that brought Lawrence to ask the question, but after giving him a faint smile, she directed her gaze forward again.

"I think we've grown too close."

Elsa was a servant of God who followed a strict set of rules to the letter.

Though that was Lawrence's impression of her, in that moment, he got a glimpse of her true self.

"I am not used to traveling. I was shaken by a sudden onset of homesickness, that's all."

Elsa originally lived a quiet life in a town called Tereo, watching over a church her father left for her. But as the world started turning a harsh gaze on the Church, she had been summoned to help with other churches here and there with managing their assets and privileges, which is how she came to a land as far north as this.

In her hometown, she apparently had three children with a man named Evan, who, in Lawrence's memory, was still a good-natured milling boy.

"Miss Holo is so sharp. I doubt I can hide my urgency to return home. But…" Elsa gave a long sigh, one that almost made her look smaller. "…I would seem cold and distant if I did not, wouldn't I?"

It was a common sight when traveling.

One could meet another person who would soon become a delightful drinking buddy; someone they could open up to and feel a deep sense of camaraderie with. But the person might suddenly leave one day, citing family reasons. To them, we are nothing more than another guest in a long stream of guests, and they have a firm routine to which they must return.

They would go back to the warm lights of their hearths, and homes filled with laughter. But those who spent their lives on the road would have to return to their inns alone. And when dawn broke again, they would move on to the next town.

Along her brief travels, Elsa must have tasted that particular flavor of loneliness.

Despite how tightly tied back her hair was, and how it seemed her astute, honey-tinted eyes saw nothing but logic and reason, Lawrence knew that she was much warmer and kinder than the average person.

The reason she found it difficult to bring up leaving was because she did not want to hurt the lone wolf.

"Should I tell her, then? I was just thinking that it was time for us to move on to the next town."

Elsa felt bad, almost as though she was making a secret deal with Lawrence while Holo was not around, so she did not reply right away. Ultimately, though, she nodded.

The smile she offered him after that was tinged by self-reproach.

"I feel like a child asking for help broaching a difficult topic."

When she had first met Lawrence, she might have brought up her leaving without much thought or warning, simply because it was the truth.

But Lawrence saw it differently.

"Learning when and how to rely on others is a part of becoming an adult, I think."

Back when he was hoping to become an independent merchant, he thought becoming an adult meant being able to solve every problem on his own.

It was not long before he learned that was, of course, an ignorant young man's hubris.

"...You act an upstanding man in your own right, so long as you're away from Miss Holo."

Elsa's exasperated yet spiteful remark earned her an honest smile from Lawrence.

"I rarely have a leg to stand on with her."

Elsa gave an exaggerated shrug, like a city girl, before ultimately smiling.

"I had not expected much when I sent you the letter. But if our unexpected reunion is anything to go by, I believe we will cross paths again," she said, not looking in Lawrence's direction. Nyohhira and Tereo were distant, and neither of them were young

181

anymore, so logical thinking dictated they would never see each other again.

Lawrence glanced at her profile before turning to face forward himself. "If anything, you should say that to Holo," he said.

He did not know if she looked at him.

As the plaza came into view, they saw that the outside of the liveliest tavern was the site for yet another contest to see who could drink the most.

The silhouette right in the middle of all the commotion, Lawrence knew without a doubt, belonged to his beloved wolf.

"I'm not sure I can find the right words," Elsa said. Despite that, once they met up with Holo and Tanya, Lawrence asked her what she planned on doing after this, just as they agreed, to which she flawlessly replied that she would be returning to Tereo, and that she had been happy to see Holo again.

Holo did not seem particularly upset about having to part ways with Elsa; she was considerably drunk, after all, and she had to keep up appearances with her pseudo-protégée, Tanya, sitting beside her.

She even promised to meet again in her premature words of parting; she was optimistic, already looking forward to their next reunion.

Tanya and Elsa returned to the church together that night, and Lawrence dragged wobbly Holo back to the inn. It seemed as though Holo was taking the sadness that came with a journey's unavoidable partings well, only with the help of alcohol, and placing it neatly at her feet.

Once the new day dawned, Holo eagerly went to join the drinking competitions early in the morning, leaving Lawrence to watch her gallant profile from the inn window as he thought about their imminent departure.

Preparing for a departure always started slow, but Lawrence's primary objective in their journey was to check up on their only daughter, Myuri. He was eager to get moving, and he knew he could not drag his feet.

Yet the reason he found himself thinking of his old mentor was likely because he was a bit apprehensive of what was to come.

It was not because they were yet to determine Myuri and Col's precise location, nor because a trying winter journey was ahead of them. It was a problem that was more down-to-earth, easier to understand, and perhaps even vexing to some.

What Lawrence was worried about was what would come after the unexpectedly brilliant and lively time they spent with Elsa and Tanya—the heavy, lingering quiet.

The reason his stray cat of a mentor rarely ever interacted with others was less because of the trade advantages it afforded him with the kinds of people he met along his travels, and more out of a more cowardly cautiousness—so that he would not be swallowed by the ebbing tide of loneliness.

His own parting with Lawrence had been sudden. When Lawrence awoke one morning, the man was gone.

The reason he had not dwelled on his unfulfilled desire to travel more with his mentor, despite being abandoned, was because he had been so desperate to survive.

When he first thought back on his mentor after he finally found his rhythm as a traveling merchant, he found that the memories had smoothed over with time, and they had settled into the recesses of his heart without any lingering pain.

Now, he understood that that was his mentor's unique way of looking out for him.

It had been so casual, but he only understood the weight of that choice after the fact. Though there was room for debate as to whether or not his crotchety old mentor's way of doing things was correct, he had indeed learned something about decisiveness in that moment. When he looked back on his life, he realized that rather than the basics of trade, this experience was the greatest lesson he had received.

So he, too, knew that he had to pay careful consideration to his traveling companion in much the same way in times like these.

Your student's still doing well for himself, Lawrence told the memory of his mentor, then downed the rest of his ale.

Outside his window, Holo—who was quite the celebrity in Salonia by now—had her arm linked through that of a sturdy-looking dock loader, and they were drinking their cups dry.

"She'll be hungover tomorrow, so I guess we'll leave the day after, or the day after that," Lawrence murmured and stood, grabbing his coat as he left the room.

Beyond the open window, Holo lifted up her empty cup and basked in the cheers and applause.

"Farewell," Elsa said briefly, and began walking down the road, headed south. It had been two days since the festival in Salonia had ended, and as the morning came once again, a reluctant air filled the town, a hint that the townsfolk would begrudgingly return to their daily lives in preparation for winter.

She had sensed that if she stayed in town one day longer, the bishop, reputed for being glib, would yet again push some troublesome affair onto her plate, so she had quite bluntly said no to any more requests for work.

Standing next to her was Tanya, who was going to be accompanying her to Tereo. Tanya kept turning around to look at Holo and wave.

At first, Holo had waved back every time, but she soon grew tired of the act and no longer raised her hand.

Yet Lawrence and Holo stood there watching until Tanya and

Elsa vanished completely; Holo stared out down the path, a whirl of emotion hidden behind her faint smile.

"What excitement that was, no?"

When they were finally gone, Holo planted her hands on her hips and spoke.

"We were surprisingly busy."

They had originally left the hot spring village of Nyohhira in order to check on their only daughter, Myuri, who had also left on a journey. But as they followed her trail, they reunited with Elsa, met Tanya, a squirrel spirit who lived on a mountain rumored to be cursed, helped merchants who had been suffocated by a tangled web of debt, and even helped a man from the distant desert—whose true nature was that of a bishop—connect with his own villagers.

All of that had made them quite well-known in Salonia, which led to him selling quite a big load of the sulfur powder, a key element in the hot springs, which Lawrence brought all the way from Nyohhira. They had also managed to replenish some of the smaller value coins that they had been lacking in as of late.

And most importantly, he had managed to spread word of their bathhouse in Nyohhira, Spice and Wolf, to the people of influence in town.

If he could tangibly harvest the fruits of a journey, then this would have been an amazing crop, but the fields after a particularly lush season often seemed starkly barren in comparison.

Even Lawrence, who was no match for Holo even in daily life, could stand toe to toe with the centuries-old wolf in terms of travel experience.

Lawrence had come up with a thorough plan so that the lonely wolf would not get swallowed by the sudden wash of negative emotions that so often caught travelers off guard.

"I suppose…'tis time for us to depart, too."

Holo raised her arms above her and stretched. She had spent the entirety of the previous day hungover, but woke up rather early this morning, looked out at the morning sun, and ate so much food, it was almost as though she was making up for the day before.

They then went to see Elsa and Tanya off, which brought them to the present moment.

Lawrence knew that the melancholy often struck out of the blue during moments like this.

"But first, there's a place we need to visit."

"Oh? Are we drinking more?"

There was a genuine glint in her eye, which brought an unwitting smile to Lawrence's face.

"No… Well, maybe."

Holo looked dubiously at Lawrence in response to his ambiguous answer, but her tail began to swish back and forth in delight at the prospect of drinking.

"Remember how the church promised they'd send a bit of wheat from their fields as thanks for mediating on the tariffs?"

"Ah, yes, I remember."

Holo sounded rather indifferent, but when she had learned that he was having wheat sent to the bathhouse every year as a reminder of their journey to that place, she was overjoyed.

She was never honest with her feelings, but that was what made her so adorable. Lawrence said to her, "We still need to decide which zone will be sending us the wheat."

"Hmm?"

"It really isn't enough for us to just ask for the best wheat every year. It might not only be an armful, but we could probably get the wheat that grows from our territory."

This was more of a formal exchange, not so one about actually getting the best wheat possible, so it was possible to call him an upstanding noble since he was the one receiving the tribute.

Lawrence looked proud, but Holo only reacted with a cold demeanor.

"It matters not where it comes from. You may pick anywhere from this land, and it will not change."

Perhaps she could not be bothered to go out into the fields, or perhaps she was not fond of the idea to cross the bridge made of boats to get there.

But Lawrence grabbed Holo's shoulders and began to guide her as he walked.

"Oh, no, we can't have that. Come on, let's go."

"Mm? Dear, what are you—goodness."

Lawrence urged an annoyed Holo on, and once they returned to the inn, they started getting ready for their departure.

They packed the cart full of things so that they would be ready to leave right after selecting their wheat field, bid good-bye to all those they had gotten to know well, then left town before noon.

Though Lawrence thought Salonia might quiet down after the festival, the town had taken on life in a different sense; all those who had spent their time idling around for the festival were now working diligently to get everything put away before winter.

That meant there were many people crossing the pontoon bridge, causing quite the sway. Holo ultimately found herself hunched over on the cart bed, holding her head in her hands.

On the opposite bank, Lawrence bought a few thinly-sliced pieces of beef shoulder from one of the food stalls, placed it on the driver's perch, and Holo at last grumpily crawled her way to the front.

"I want wine," she said as she tore into the beef, still a bit pink in the middle, but Lawrence ignored her as he gazed up at the sky, urging the cart forward.

People shouldering farming tools and carts filled with stacks of straw rushed by them in either direction, but what stood out the most were the girls walking boldly, carrying massive scythes that were bigger than them.

Once the fortress tower came into view, they saw that patches were starting to be harvested from what was a perfect, unbroken blanket of crop just a few days earlier.

"Mm! The delicious aroma of wheat."

There was a hint of dust, but accompanied by the rich scent of wheat on the calm breeze.

Holo, licking her fingers clean after devouring the meat, allowed the wind to brush gently past her cheek—she seemed perfectly happy again.

"Pick out a spot that looks like it's producing good wheat. You can choose wherever you want."

"'Twill only be from an arm's width, though, no?"

"Pick wherever you want from an arm's width."

Holo turned a cold gaze toward Lawrence, but her wolf ears were twitching happily beneath her hood.

As they conversed and made their way toward the fortress, once home to a hero who was said to have defeated a great serpent that lived on this plain, they found the gates were wide open, and crowds of people were streaming in and out.

"This reminds me of the past."

Holo once ruled over the wheat harvest in a village called Pasloe. It was a village Lawrence had frequented for his trade; it had been a lively little place, since a festival was always held around harvest time.

Though there was no proper festival held here, it being a fortress meant that the location came equipped with a storehouse and a central square, and so at this time of year, when all the farmers were hard at work, Lawrence had heard that it took on the spirit of a festival in its own right.

Some time later, Salonia saw the harvest begin in the area around the fortress. At the same time, wheat that had been harvested a bit earlier was brought in to be husked. Lawrence guessed that it was going to be even livelier than he imagined.

That was because song and drink were easily passed around in places of monotonous labor.

"Oh ho! Now this is a good festival!"

Lawrence smiled as Holo, sitting atop the driver's perch, began to delight in the sounds of singing and the smell of smoke from cookfires.

Farmers and children hopped onto the cart bed without warning along the way, likely thinking he was one of the passing merchants. Once they entered the fort and the familiar assistant priest, who was overseeing the harvesting and the husking, saw Lawrence and Holo, his eyes went wide with surprise.

"I'm sorry to intrude while you're so busy. We came to choose the land for our wheat."

The assistant priest gave them an exasperated look, but he had no time to be angry with them.

"Pick whichever land you like. And feel free to watch the husking."

The offer to watch was a roundabout way for him to ask them to help with the task, and Holo was surprisingly keen.

"You may use my horse to help, too."

The assistant priest drew up his shoulders and immediately called out to the villagers.

Lawrence pretended not to notice the little glare he thought the horse gave him now that it had been saddled with the role of pack animal.

When Holo and Lawrence came to the field together, they saw that the harvest had progressed rather far in the fields by the fortress. People were planting stakes in the ground and gathering all the harvested wheat together to be dried.

"They only started harvesting yesterday, or the day before, but they've already gathered so much."

In the distance they spotted young girls with long pigtails, deftly wielding their massive scythes. Just like when it came to grape stomping for wine-making, harvesting the wheat was the time for the local girls to shine.

"Shall we take a little look around?"

"It truly does not matter where we go," Holo said, yet she still took Lawrence's hand and set off with light steps.

They occasionally took walks together in Nyohhira, but the village was mostly comprised of narrow paths and a steamy haze, and a step out of the village brought them to a deep wood. It was not since their old journey that they had been able to walk the plains with such extensive vistas as this.

Holo hummed as she walked, smiling at the sight of bewildered frogs and rabbits that had been chased from their sleeping spots among the wheat.

"Should I still see if I can make that fortress ours?"

If they were to turn around on their little footpath, they would see said fortress standing dignified atop the hill. They could take leisurely walks along this path whenever they wanted if they lived there. And people would refer to them as lord and lady as a bonus, making it the peak of their progress in life.

But Holo cackled, her laugh sounding almost like a cough as her shoulders shuddered, and she brushed off some scraps of straw that clung to her shoulder as she said, "Stone buildings are much too cold for me."

"You're right. We're both getting old, anyway."

Holo gave him a dubious look and patted his back.

"But that rambunctious Myuri would be delighted if we were to make the castle ours."

That was their only daughter, who would make swords out of sticks and eagerly pretend to play the hero.

But Lawrence found himself taking Holo's offhand remark into serious consideration.

His daughter, who used to constantly beg for his company, now no longer wanted anything to do with him as she grew. And she was also perfectly old enough for it to be possible that she had gotten married off in a land he knew nothing about. He thought that perhaps he liked it better if they could get this stone fortress for her, so that she could indulge in playing knight to her heart's content.

As he seriously considered it, he felt a cold stare on him, and he turned to look at the source.

"You fool," Holo said with a sigh.

Lawrence looked reluctantly at the fortress one more time, then dropped his shoulders.

"You never know when to give up, do you?"

"...We have a lot of very nice things because of that, though."

"You argue simply to argue." Holo reached out with a small hand to pinch Lawrence's cheek and a delighted smile crossed her face. "And what about here for land?"

With the opposite hand, Holo pointed to the corner of one zone.

It was beside a small hedgerow, planted there either to alleviate the wind or for firewood, or perhaps even as a way to demarcate the zone.

"You think it grows best in places like that?" Lawrence asked, impressed; he was a complete novice when it came to field work. Maybe the leaves that fell in the winter served as good fertilizer.

Holo gave a slight shrug. "'Tis simply a spot easy to find."

"…"

Lawrence looked at Holo in mild disappointment, and his wife, once known as the wisewolf, glared at him.

"Do not underestimate places that are easy to find. The fields change more than you know. Those who till the land change, too. But markers like those stay the same for decades, centuries. When you found that old map in the castle, you must have found some markers that had not changed for a long time, though the shape of the fields themselves change."

"Now that you mention it, we were there when people were arguing over land boundaries along our old journey. We needed your wisdom to solve that one, too."

Even if it had been preserved in writing, differences in interpretation and boundaries blurred over the years made for the seed of future dispute.

What Holo had proposed to those villagers in order to avoid such conflict in the future was rather violent—to bring their children to the boundary line, and pinch their cheeks as hard as they could. The children would never forget that moment, and it would prove the standard for when they quarreled over the boundary again in the future.

That said, they could not drag along a poor local child and pinch their cheeks for an arm width's amount of land, so hedgerows like these served as a good marker.

I see, of course she is the wisewolf, the one who rules over wheat, Lawrence thought, but Holo looked up at him with a hard stare.

"You made it so the wheat would be sent to Nyohhira for decades—no, centuries to come, yes?"

Lawrence had asked the church to send them wheat as part of the landowning rights that they held, not as a bit of thanks.

This was where they could use the power of tax history, an unbroken chain recorded since the beginning of the era of humanity, and the method easily kept Holo's longevity, one that far surpassed human lives, in mind.

That methodology seemed a bit ridiculous for such a small portion of land, just an armful, but it had been necessary for Lawrence.

That was because it was the centuries-old wisewolf, the one that would live much longer than Lawrence himself, the one that looked exactly like the pretty young girl she was when he first met her.

Lawrence made it so that the memories of their journey would always reach Holo in Nyohhira in the form of wheat.

"You could have picked a better parting gift," she said, patting her hand on his chest.

And oddly, Lawrence found comfort in how she always seemed one step ahead. "I can never win with you, can I?"

"No, you cannot," she chuckled.

Lawrence took her hand and spun her around.

"Now then, let's put this zone down on parchment, and help with husking and whatnot in the meanwhile."

"Do not hurt your back again."

"Ah."

"Well, if that happened, I suppose I would not mind. We would have to remain in this lively town, and I will simply have to continue drinking."

"They're probably going to start asking you to pay if you did that."

Holo was famous in Salonia, and her spirited drinking earned her free booze here and there, but she was dangerously close to overstaying her welcome.

"All you do is think of stingy profits."

"When I think about how much I've spent on alcohol for you, I start to wonder if we should've made a vineyard instead of a bathhouse."

"You fool!" Holo took the hand she had intwined with Lawrence's and smacked his back. "Then we would be stuck drinking wine all the time!"

What she said did not exactly sound like a joke, so Lawrence had no choice but to stand down.

"And all sorts of drinks find their way to Nyohhira," she added. "Everything tastes good whilst soaking in the baths."

Elsa would surely scold her again if she heard that, but Lawrence knew he was partially responsible for always treating her to a drink, wanting to see her happy.

"We should see if we can find an alcohol spring instead."

"'Twould be most ideal, yes."

Even though their motives were likely not quite on the same page, Lawrence did not point that out; he only tugged her hand to lead her back to the fortress with a shake of his head.

Songs sung as monotonous manual labor was being done were repetitions of easy-to-remember stanzas and melodies. Both Lawrence and Holo quickly learned the tune, took their own tools for husking—two sticks connected together by a string— and joined in the villagers singing as they worked the wheat.

Holo had spent centuries in Pasloe, but she only ever helped with the harvest work herself a few times in the distant past; she had simply watched in the times after that.

The reason she quickly gave up husking the wheat was less out of boredom and more out of her inherent curiosity—she wanted to see what the other work was like.

She joined in with the ones who bit into the harvested wheat to see if it had dried completely and helped out with picking chaff and other contaminants from the wheat in a big washtub. There had been a particular trick to shaking out the washtub, and the other girls there giggled at her as she ended up shaking her hips more than the tub.

The harvesting work in the fortress would last for more than one or two days. And so, instead of persevering throughout the entire thing, people often changed jobs or stepped out briefly, giving the sense that they would carry on with this work in a relaxed manner for a long time.

Just as Lawrence found himself getting lost in the rhythm of the monotonous work, one of the villagers asked to switch with him, and he reluctantly handed over his husking sticks.

"Now, then." He glanced around the area to find Holo missing from the lively castle garden. He asked around and learned that once she was done helping pick out bad-quality grains from a mountain of the wheat, she had gone into the main house.

Though it was getting closer to the height of autumn, it was still rather hot when the sun was high in the sky. Lawrence wondered if she had worn herself out and was taking a rest since she had such a terrible hangover the day before. Holo was typically slothful, so she would sometimes push herself too far when it came to work like this and suddenly run out of energy.

Despite his worry, Lawrence thought she was likely all right if she had taken a break of her own accord, so he decided to wrap up the matter on the delivery of their goods. He fished out some parchment from their things and made his way into the great room, where the assistant priest was watching over everything.

"Have you chosen a field?"

The assistant priest, who had been writing down the amount of wheat harvested and how the harvest was progressing in charcoal on a large wooden board leaning up against one of the walls in the great room, turned to Lawrence, clearly not bothered by the charcoal smeared on his face.

The church in Salonia presently owned the privileges to the land once ruled over by one called the Hero Voragine, but owning those rights did not necessarily mean things would always go smoothly.

There was still the matter of managing the day-to-day activities on the land, bringing someone in to manage the harvest period, making sure it was collected for taxes, being conscious of the worst and best of the harvest, and trying to avoid being scammed or subject to any injustices.

The assistant priest, who seemed to have been left in charge of all those things, had been very kind to Lawrence and his entourage when they came to visit in relation to the tariff troubles. That was perhaps because he had been hoping to hand off some of the work to Lawrence, but when he saw just how exhausted he looked, he had a feeling that might happen.

"Yes, we found a nice spot, so I came to inform you."

Aside from the board, where the assistant priest had written down reports that came in from the villagers and the apprentice clergy boys diligently copied the sheer volume of numbers down onto paper, there was a rough map of the territory drawn in charcoal, and Lawrence pointed to it.

"The field right next to the first shrubs southwest from the fortress."

"There, yes. I'm glad you picked a spot easy to find. All the

196

quarrelling over zone divisions causes us headaches throughout the year."

The easy-to-find point that Holo had indicated had apparently been very important.

The assistant priest took two of the deeds the bishop had given Lawrence, then turned to the apprentice clergy boy and named several villagers and ordered him to write down a zone about a pace wide where those villagers' locations intersected.

"These privileges become yours in God's name." The assistant priest looked between the two pieces of parchment and handed one back to Lawrence as he spoke.

"Glory be to God," Lawrence said.

The assistant priest exhaled in a way that could be either taken as a sigh or a sign of agreement, then rolled his head around his neck and shoulders.

"Thank you for all of your hard work," Lawrence added.

"I wish I could have taken a dip in the hot springs you built in Salonia."

"You're always welcome at our bathhouse," Lawrence said with a smile.

The assistant priest grimaced. "Aren't the hot springs in Nyohhira supposed to be a secret? I heard only archbishops are allowed there."

"That's a bit of an exaggeration. But even if it were true, then I suppose we would be welcoming you in the near future."

Though he was young, the assistant priest was canny enough to grow a beard to give himself a mature and dignified air. His lips stretched into a grin under his messy whiskers.

"I will be sure to send the wheat your way every year."

"You have my thanks."

Lawrence was certain this assistant priest would reach great heights and become a regular at their bathhouse.

As that thought crossed his mind, he rolled up the parchment and tucked it away in his pocket.

"Where has your wife gone, by the way? Do you have any plans for the rest of the day?"

The assistant priest seemed keen to offer they stay here for the night, but as they stood here speaking, there was a line outside the door of people waiting to report to him.

Lawrence replied briefly, "We're hoping to leave before sunset and follow the river downstream."

"I see. Lovely."

The smile on his face suggested he was relieved there was one less thing he had to worry about on his plate.

"Thank you."

Lawrence gave a nod, which the assistant priest returned with a polite bow, and he was already back into work mode. Lawrence left the great room, sliding past all the people waiting in line, then planted his hands on his hips with a sigh.

"Now, where has that Holo gone?"

The old fortress was not small by any means. Though the sun was still high in the sky, the light did not reach the depths of the building, and a dreary ambiance settled in the darkest corners.

He doubted she had gotten lost and was crying somewhere in this big fortress, but he did wonder if she had suddenly gotten emotional out of the blue.

Lawrence had brought Holo to the lively harvesting work area so that she would not be suddenly overwhelmed by the gaping hole left by the busy and exciting time spent with Elsa and Tanya. Jumping from the roof of a five-story building would surely cause great bodily harm, but jumping down to the four-story building next door, then to the three-story one, then the two-story store-house and *then* onto the street would make it possible to walk home.

He thought it would be nice to take a breather with the lively harvest workers, then return to the river and take a boat downstream. They would be awash in the lively atmosphere—not just the shanties sung by the captain, but calls from those pulling the boat downstream, and excited greetings from those traversing the roads that ran alongside the river. There were also regular checkpoints built along the river, so they would surely find vendors in those places. And then, once they came to the port on the sea at the mouth of the river, that would provide even further relief.

Elsa would surely tell Lawrence that he was coddling Holo again, but he believed it was his life's work to do whatever he could to help her.

And as of late, Lawrence had grown fond of her demure squirming as he catered to her needs.

He searched the building with those thoughts in mind, and eventually heard that Holo had ventured into the third-floor storage area with a mug of booze in hand.

He passed the women sitting around the hearth on the second floor doing the mer ...ng, stepped through men who were reattaching polished scythe blades to their handles, weaved through children sitting on the stairs, picking out whatever looked edible from the poor-quality grains, and headed for the third floor.

There were plenty of people busily going to and fro on the third floor, lending to a constant buzz throughout the area; Lawrence doubted she was here moping.

But as he wandered, lost, not sure exactly where the storage room was, he saw four men emerge carrying a pot meant for making food for all the people who had come to work—it was big enough for a fully-grown adult to use as a bath. Behind them was Holo, a stack of three pots on her head and a spoon large enough to hold a baby under her left arm.

"…What are you doing?"

Lawrence's eyes widened when he saw her peculiar dress; if someone told him that she was wearing a costume for a festival, he would believe them. Holo, carrying herself in a strange fashion so that the pots on her head would not fall, jerked her chin toward the storage room.

"Do not just stand there. The spears for roasting the meat are in there. Bring them out. Put all the firewood and charcoal you can find into the tub!"

That was all Holo said to him as she followed the men carrying the large pot, making sure the ones on her head didn't topple over.

Sitting by the door to the storage was a half-drunk mug of ale; she had likely been resting there when the men came by, and so she had jumped back into work.

The reason she was so enthused was likely because she was expecting to get a tasty meal out of it.

He had fully assumed she would be sitting by a window or in a dark corner of the storage room, so he was relieved to see that this was not the case. He did as he was told and carried as much as he could bear down the stairs.

Merchants who came while the villagers were working, aiming to purchase this year's wheat at its peak, also came by, and the alcohol and meat they brought made their lunch break feel just like a mini festival.

A whole pig had been skewered and was being roasted over a makeshift stove in the garden. Thick plumes of smoke billowed into the air whenever a drop of fat landed on the hot coals and wafted over the people as they sliced off thin pieces with a knife as big as an adult's arm. The meat was then messily placed on

201

some bread and handed around to the others. Holo, soot staining her cheek, added plenty of mustard onto one of the smoky pieces of pork before biting into it.

Her tail was fully fluffed under her clothes in her eagerness, but no one noticed in all the hubbub.

Lawrence used his own finger to wipe the soot from her cheek, and bit into his own portion.

So much meat had been shaved off the pig, yet despite the fact that it had been worked nearly down to the bone, it kept spinning above the smoldering coals.

It was then that Lawrence took his horse's reins in hand, nudged a reluctant Holo, and they left the fortress together.

Outside the fortress were people lying in the grass, taking a break after their meal, and children chasing away the birds that had come in search of grains of wheat that had not quite made it to the fortress with peals of laughter.

Holo was lying down not on the driver's perch, but in the cart bed. She basked in the sun as it still hung high in the sky, her ears flitting about, listening to the commotion, and patted her stomach in satisfaction.

"Don't fall asleep yet," Lawrence said as he drove the cart forward.

"Fool," came the quiet reply, but her speech was already mumbled. "*Yaaawn*... Where are we going now?"

She was still lying down as she spoke. She was clearly ready to fall asleep.

With a shrug, Lawrence replied, "We'll head back to the river near town and take a boat downstream."

"Mm..."

"You can sleep once we get on the boat. Try to stay awake until we get there. I'd hate for you to fall into the river because you nodded off."

He didn't hear her call him a fool, so he glanced over his shoulder to see she had curled up and was sleeping soundly.

"My goodness," he said with a small smile, readjusting the grip on the reins and urging the cart forward.

Everything had gone according to plan so far.

He hid that thought beneath his smile as they traversed the road they came in on, and when they arrived at the river port, Holo woke up in a better mood than he thought.

"Ah, what excellent horsemanship," Holo remarked.

She spoke up after stepping on board the boat because she was impressed by the skill of the rider that would be delivering the horses of all the boat's passengers downstream. There were about ten horses in total, and the rider had them dashing ahead.

"Will we be retrieving the cart on the way back?" She glanced back at the boat tied to the back of the boat they were presently riding on and asked Lawrence. That particular boat was filled with their belongings, not the cart itself.

"No. We'll be hitting up a port town once we reach the end of the river, and we'll be able to get the same kind of cart when we get there. It costs a lot of money to bring it with us, you see."

"Mm. You are clever, as always. How convenient."

It was likely because he had money orders in mind—something that let a person walk around without any coins in their pocket—which led him to think of something similar.

"Oh, right. I need to tell you something. Just in case the boat tips over."

"Hmm?"

"I don't care if we lose the sulfur and whatever else. Just don't ever let go of this bag, okay?'

One bag, purposely separated from the others on the cart, now sat at Lawrence's and Holo's feet.

Inside was a pouch stuffed full of small coins they had gotten in Salonia.

"You fool. I will not sink to the bottom of the river with such a thing. If the boat tips over, we should try to save this instead," Holo said, patting a small barrel.

It was whisky they had gotten a significant discount for in Salonia—the drink had been nicknamed *fire water*.

"We will be able to reach port without drowning if we drink the contents and hold onto it, no?"

"…So long as you don't black out."

"Water is essential for sobering up."

Despite his exasperation, Lawrence decided he would quite enjoy seeing Holo drifting happily down the river.

"Right, well, we're off."

"Mm."

After making the final loading checks, the boatman undid the rope on the docks, dipped the pole into the water, and the boat slowly parted from the riverbank. Altogether, there were six boats headed for the sea, and each one was filled with people and possessions. Lawrence and Holo had gotten special treatment for doing such good work and earning fame in Salonia, which meant they got the front boat all to themselves.

As he thought back on how different things were now compared to when he was a traveling merchant before meeting Holo, he could not help the smile that crossed his face.

"What is it?"

They sat on a thick blanket of wool, Holo nestled between Lawrence's legs, ready to fall asleep at any moment, and she felt him laugh on her back, and so she asked.

"I was just thinking about how luxurious our journey has been."

Holo's reddish-amber eyes went wide before creating half-moons to complement her contented smile. "Journeys such as this one suit me best."

"Indeed."

He placed his hand on her head, and she rubbed her head against it, demanding that he pet her more. Her wolf's dignity was nowhere to be found.

The weather was nice, and since it had not rained in quite a while, the river was calm and gently carried the boats downstream. The afternoon sun was warm, the faint song of the boatman filled the air around them, and the lively working sounds of those in the fields along the river were a gentle tickle in the ear.

While this indulgence was rather different from the excitement of a roaring fire, it was accompanied by a joy that came with traveling—much like eating one ripe grape at a time and savoring each bite.

Holo soon fell asleep again, her lips occasionally moving with leisure as she dreamed.

Lawrence wanted to say that everything was going as planned, but after they drifted for a while down the river, he realized that the boat was moving a lot slower than he had anticipated. He started to worry that they wouldn't reach the coast by nightfall; when he asked the boatman, the boatman explained that they would have had to take an early-morning boat in order to reach the port by evening, and that the only boats departing after noon that could make the journey were ones during melt season, or when it had rained upstream.

The boatman suggested they get a room at an inn in the large checkpoint just before they reach the sea.

Holo would surely assume that the body of water she saw when she awoke was the ocean, meaning she might scold him for his poor judgment. But he could not change the flow of the river, and the boatman told him that the checkpoint at which they planned on mooring was a rather lively river port, so Lawrence adjusted his expectations—perhaps it was not all that bad to spend the night at a nice riverside inn.

Warmed by the sun, Lawrence took Holo, her soot smell and all, into his embrace and closed his eyes. The next thing he knew, it was sundown.

They were still on the river when they awoke, so Holo gave Lawrence an earful, just as he expected, yet she watched over the buzz of activity unique to the river port with delight.

Lawrence took only their valuables from the ship, such as the pouch full of coins, had a branch from one of Salonia's companies watch after their things, and secured a room for himself and Holo in the meantime.

Rumors of their exploits had reached the port already, so that had been easy.

There seemed to still be quite a bit of distance to the ocean; so when he turned west, to where the ocean was supposed to be, Lawrence found himself faced with a terrifyingly vast open sky, a sensation only amplified by the featureless geography. The clear indigo of the night sky mixing with the fiery sunset was a stunning sight. As they sat at one of the riverside taverns, Holo had been so entranced by it that she almost forgot to drink any of the ale she had been served.

One could see a similar sight in Nyohhira by climbing to the top of a mountain, but being so close to the sea, which was essentially nothingness, the sky most certainly felt much bigger.

In previous travels, both Lawrence and Holo had gotten to see the sea, but the scenery changed with the time and place. Surely, once they reached the end of the river and came to the port, the sun setting over the sea would look much different from this.

"Your food's getting cold," Lawrence said, biting into his skewered trout, but Holo simply continued to stare at the setting sun, not even looking at him or nodding in response. It was rare that she was expressionless like this in front of him.

The way she looked made her seem entirely defenseless, as though every layer of her heart, right down to the thin film around her core, had been peeled away.

It was a strange expression—one that was not quite sad, yet hard to call optimistic—and Lawrence was certain that he would never be able to understand the feelings behind it. Those emotions belonged only to those who had lived for centuries, only when experiencing a sight that had not changed in hundreds of years.

And Lawrence had a feeling, too, that they were not happy feelings for her.

All he could do at times like these was just stay by her side and understand the plan he had painstakingly laid out to bring Holo joy was nothing before the overwhelming forces of nature.

He stared at the smudge on the table, created by a tear that had suddenly spilled from Holo's expressionless eyes, as he swallowed the tender, salty meat of his trout.

The only reason he could still taste it was not only because he knew how to show his understanding for the world's providence after becoming an adult. It was because now that his life was half over, he was starting to accept—reluctantly in defeat, even—that in the face of the immutable truths of the world, one could not stand one's ground, only let the flow take over.

"Your fish is getting cold," Lawrence said again, though not out of concern.

It was his way of showing defiance in the face of the flow of the immutable truths of the world.

Holo, standing in a perfectly still, mirror-like lake, could only find the shore by the help of those who boldly stepped in and caused ripples.

Though there was still some distance to the shore, when she turned to look at Lawrence, a relieved smile crossed her face.

"Yes, it smells good. 'Twould be a waste to let it go cold."

There were glimpses of unease behind Holo's expression, like she was taking in the scent in a dream. But when she, at last, hesitantly bit into her fish, she finally understood that this was not a dream.

"I think they'll be playing music soon."

Lawrence gestured with his chin to an open stall by the river, where some traveling musicians were preparing their instruments to busk. At the checkpoint, visible from where they sat, boats came in one after the other, and out of them came a stream of people on land eager to end their day with a cold pint.

Unlike cities encased in walls, the rules in riverside ports were lax. As he looked out at the lack of open seats, he could easily imagine how the lively chatter lasted well into the night every day.

"The fun's just beginning," Lawrence said.

Holo, consuming half her trout in a single bite, head-first, guts and all, looked up at him as the bones crunched between her teeth.

After swallowing, she devoured the rest of the fish with her second bite and licked her lips.

"I'm going to burp," she said.

Lawrence frowned at her, and she gave him an ironic, lopsided grin before pointing her skewer at him.

"Not because of the fish. Because of you."

Before Lawrence could ask what she meant, Holo took a large swig of ale, placed her wooden mug down on the table with a satisfied hum, and immediately ordered more.

"Of course 'tis because of you," she repeated, and finally belched loudly in quite an unladylike fashion.

Truly satisfied, as though she had managed to dislodge a bone from her throat, she turned to look at him.

"I spend all my days subject to your doting, and then I find that those days have come to an end."

Holo reached for a new trout skewer, bringing it up to her lips in a kiss, then mercilessly bit into it.

"Thus begins again a journey of *two* lonely people."

Despite how packed her cheeks were with fish, she didn't let a single morsel spill out.

After a gulp, she brought up some more ale to her lips.

"You brought me all the way to those fields when you could have simply selected whatever you liked. We took part in the lively harvesting activities, then took a boat down the river toward the sea. And now look at you; how stingy you were about traveling by land when we left Nyohhira. Hmm... But perhaps you've simply injured your back, which would explain the stiffness."

Holo smiled, genuinely delighted, before letting out a sigh.

When she turned to look back at the sky, the final vestiges of the setting sun threatening to be swallowed by night, her face was no longer expressionless.

"I know you are doting on me because you are worried, giving me constant joy in our travels so that I do not succumb to despair."

Her eyelids lowered, then shut as she tilted her head, fondly reliving her memories, before opening her eyes again.

"And what joy does it bring me. Even the ones that do not quite hit their mark and make me irritated."

Lawrence raised his hands in an admission of defeat, and Holo nodded to him like a benevolent queen.

"Every day I travel with you is a joy, thanks to that. But 'tis strange, because I find the dull moments just as delightful."

"Uh…hmm?"

Lawrence murmured in response, and Holo asked a passing tavern girl for more meat.

"I never noticed it when we were in the bathhouse, much less when I first met you."

Holo placed the skewer in her mouth and began nibbling on it.

"Even the sadness, the loneliness, the overwhelming pain I feel in the quiet moments between journeys brings me joy."

"That's, um…huh?"

Holo gave a shy smile in response to Lawrence's bewilderment.

"Isn't it strange? What is sad is sad, and what is painful is painful, but all the ups and downs, and even the depths of the abyss, where I sit with my knees to my chest—I find delight in it all."

She was clearly not saying this to bring Lawrence peace of mind, so he could only watch her, completely blank faced. Pork sausage was brought to their table, and Holo surprisingly cut Lawrence a piece, so he slowly brought it to his mouth.

The bursting fat was sweet, and he found himself desperately wanting a sip of ale.

"'Twas only after meeting you that I learned to enjoy everything life has to offer, I think," she said, biting into the sausage with an innocence that rivaled her daughter, Myuri. "I suppose 'tis like finding bitter ale delicious. So…mm. I will not tell you to stop doting on me. In a way, by marrying me, you made a promise to dote on me for the rest of your life."

Despite how bluntly she spoke the words, having her state it in such a clear manner only made the former merchant happy, considering how he understood the joy in another keeping to a contract.

"And so, I have a request for you. Days filled with joy do bring me joy, yes, but I want to feel the full range of sadness when I am by your side, as well. I want to enjoy whatever emotion comes to me when our exciting days spent with that vexing girl and the fluffy, annoying squirrel suddenly come to an end. I want to find delight in sadness that has no outlet, in finding a spot to sulk and mope."

That seemed unhealthy to Lawrence, but what told him it was not was how he saw the minstrels finish tuning their instruments. Each headed for different taverns—their own territory, presumably—greeted the customers, and began taking song requests.

At some point in his travels, Lawrence had learned one thing: Songs played for money were not meant to rile up a crowd—they were sad tunes.

"Because I know I am safe when I cry beside you."

Living was not a series of constant joys. But that did not mean it was pain that constantly plagued faulty people, as the clergy spoke of it.

Having both joy and despair at opposite ends of the spectrum meant that they could find delight in the world in all different shades and hues.

"Shall we request a song?"

Holo called the minstrel over and jerked her chin at Lawrence. Lawrence, completely at Holo's whim, hurriedly pulled out some coins and placed them in the minstrel's hand.

"What sort of tune shall I play for you?"

This minstrel was unlike the ones who came to Nyohhira—he was on the shifty side, quite possibly the type to commit petty thievery.

Holo said to the minstrel, "Play us the most upbeat tune you have. One that will deafen me."

The minstrel's eyes widened in surprise before a dauntless smile crossed his face.

It was his way of telling her that he was happy to take on the challenge.

Fortunately, a crowd of sailors had just thronged into the tavern.

It was the perfect opportunity to spark the crowd.

"Lend me your ears! This tune will be the envy of legends!"

He strummed his instrument, and the customers turned to look.

When he began to stomp his feet, the excitable members of the crowd began to join in.

There was visible concern on a serving girl's face. She was likely worried about whether or not the platform over the river would hold. The stakes that sprouted from the river began to creak under the pressure, causing little ripples in the water.

As the raucous uproar grew, Lawrence and Holo instead found a quiet moment between them.

"I believe my ears will be ringing by the time we go to sleep tonight," Lawrence said, exhausted.

"What? The one thing I can find no joy in is a hangover," replied Holo calmly.

Lawrence shot her a look—perhaps she need not drink so much, then. But she gave him a pure smile and tilted her head; she deliberately downed her ale before asking for another mug.

Lawrence and Holo's journey would continue.

The hour would grow late, and no matter how cold the wind blew, they would not be alone.

And the sun would rise in the east, yet again, on the morrow.

AFTERWORD

Hello, this is Isuna Hasekura. It's been a year and nine months since the last volume, so I apologize for the wait. I've been busy writing *Wolf and Parchment* and busy with jobs relating to *Spice and Wolf VR*, so *Spice and Wolf* has not vanished from my life completely, but I was not actually working on any manuscripts. I really need to get to work…

That said, I put some themes I had been wanting to use to good use this time around, had Elsa and Tanya doing a lot of work, so as the author, I am very pleased (I really hope you, the readers, enjoy it). I would call this a short story collection, and I believe you will find things that are more fantasy-esque than in the original series, so it was a lot of fun to write.

Now let me tell you some of the things that served as inspiration for the stories. Spoilers.

The Gem of the Sea and Wolf: I've always wanted to write about the coral fishing from the Maghreb region, so I did. They really do throw metal hooks into the water and then reel them in. In present-day society, I think we would be scared of messing up the sea floor.

Summer's Harvest and Wolf: The mushroom in this chapter is the *Xylaria polymorpha*, or the dead man's fingers. Look it up online, and you'll see why Myuri was so shocked!

An Old Hound's Sigh and Wolf: The tracks left by the great serpent are what we call cropmarks. You'll find lots of aerial photographs if you search that term online, and it is cool to see exactly what they look like.

You won't find much on those things in documents related to medieval Europe, so it is difficult to just wait until I happen across something interesting. But I am certain there are more things that would suit a fantasy world, so I have a feeling *Spring Log* will continue for the time to come (I know the last chapter felt very final, but it isn't. Just in case).

Be patient, and more will come.

I have some space left... This is very recent, but I have been really craving the American-style donuts from Yamazaki Baking, so I searched all of the stores in my neighborhood but came up empty-handed. *Maybe Daily Yamazaki will have them!* I thought, and hopped on the train to the closest branch, but again, nothing!

Maybe they don't sell them in the summertime. Nothing beats how moist they are, the aggressive presence of sugar and oil. Oh, American-style donuts! If I talk about how much weight I've gained in my next afterword, then please rest easy knowing that I managed to find them. Until next time.

Isuna Hasekura

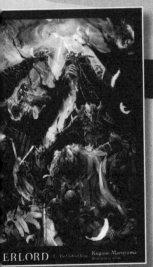

RESCUE CONTROL MAP

(from the mission control whiteboard)

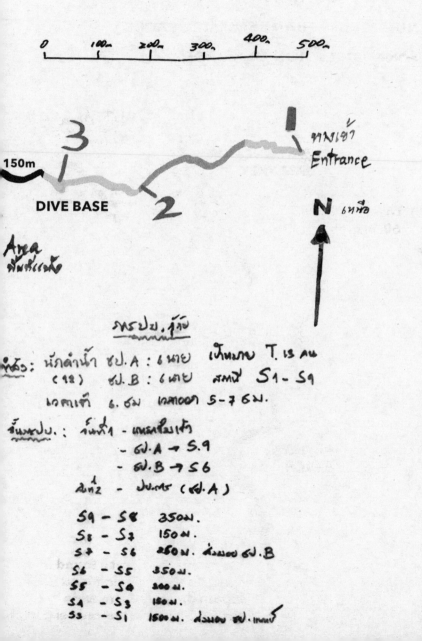